WILD LOVE
KINGDOM OF WOLVES

C.R. JANE

MILA YOUNG

DEDICATION

For all the wild women and men we love!

JOIN OUR READERS' GROUP

Stay up to date with C.R. Jane by joining her Facebook readers' group, C.R.'s Fated Realm. Ask questions, get first looks at new books/series, and have fun with other book lovers!

Join C.R. Jane's Group

Join Mila Young's Wicked Readers Group to chat directly with Mila and other readers about her books, enter giveaways, and generally just have loads of fun!

Join Mila's Group

KINGDOM OF WOLVES SERIES
FROM C.R. JANE AND MILA YOUNG

Wild Moon
Wild Heart
Wild Girl
Wild Love
Wild Soul

These stories are set in the Kingdom of Wolves shared world, but our Wild series will follow Rune's continuing story with her alphas.

WILD LOVE

Real Wolves Bite...

The stranger in town whispers promises of heaven... but in his eyes, all I see is chaos.

For most of my life I'd been cursed. Trapped in a gilded cage by my fated mate...
Everything changed when I escaped and met two men who gave me their hearts.

Wilder and Daxon are my everything... even if they don't see eye to eye on sharing me.

Things should have been amazing.
But maybe I wasn't meant for a happy ending.

My world is falling apart. Between losing friends, more

deaths in town, mysteries I can't solve, and one of my lovers betraying me....

It feels like I'm losing everything.

Amidst all of this, there's a stranger in town who's set his sights on me, and I can't figure him out. He's everywhere I am, and the problem is, I can't seem to resist him.

Loving two men has been hard enough.

But maybe all wild loves require sacrifice to keep them.

The question is...how far am I willing to go to keep mine?

■■■■■■■■■■■■■■

I Knew You Were Trouble (Taylor's Version)
Taylor Swift

All I Want
Kodaline

Sparks
Coldplay

Needed Me
Rihanna

Bad Habits
Ed Sheeran

jealousy, jealousy
Olivia Rodrigo

Easy On Me
Adele

Nothing New
Taylor Swift, Phoebe Bridgers

Ghost
Justin Bieber

To Build A Home
The Cinematic Orchestra, Patrick Watson

Happier Than Ever
Billy Eilish

Listen to the Spotify Playlist here.

WILD SOUL
BOOK 4

Real Wolves Bite. Continue the Wild series...

Get your copy of Wild Soul today!

WILD SERIES

Wild Moon

Wild Heart

Wild Girl

Wild Love

Wild Soul

PROLOGUE
RUNE

His teeth ripped into the throat of the hunter struggling in his arms. He lifted his head towards the heavens, an ecstatic groan falling from his mouth as he savored the taste of the hunter's blood. He buried his face into his victim's neck once again, slurping loudly, the sound combining with the cries coming from some of the still dying men around him.

He took one last draw of blood before dropping the now dead hunter to the ground. I winced at the way the hunter's head hit the ground, even though he was dead...and obviously wouldn't feel it. Add in the fact that his goal had been to kill me, and I shouldn't be feeling any sympathy for him.

What I was experiencing was probably just nerves... from the fact that I was standing in the middle of a scene from a horror movie.

The ground was stained crimson with the blood of everyone he slaughtered. The bodies were piled up everywhere, their unseeing eyes staring up at the sky in a way that would be carved into my mind forever. I took a step backward and my shoe sunk into the sodden grass, which was soaked with blood, not water.

It was hard to differentiate my feelings at the moment with my heart threatening to beat out of my chest. Was it fear? Disgust? Lust...

He stood there in front of me, not a speck of blood on his pristine white shirt. No blood anywhere on him actually, other than the blood staining his lips and teeth. I absentmindedly wondered how that was even possible.

His chest was heaving and his eyes were glowing as he stared at me, hunger and madness pouring out of him.

How had I missed it before? He'd been so charming. Every person in town had loved him...wanted to be his best friend. I'd fallen under his spell just as hard. With everything going on with Daxon and Wilder, he'd managed to slip in somehow.

I'd been a fool.

I should have remembered that the most dangerous things come in the prettiest packages. Hadn't I been taught that lesson a million times before?

He began to walk towards me, and I trembled as I stood there, knowing that I should run but feeling paralyzed in place.

He didn't stop walking until he was standing right in front of me, looking down at me with possession and hunger, like his existence began and ended with me.

I felt owned at this moment, like it wasn't possible to belong to anyone else when this creature was in my presence.

He grazed his hand softly across my cheek, and I shivered, the sensation dripping down my spine and across every inch of me.

"Are you ready to belong to me? I'm the only one who truly would burn the world for you, little darling."

A soft keen ripped from my throat as his thumb traced my lips.

His eyes began to glow, a crimson ring replacing the brilliant blue I'd grown used to seeing. He smiled, and my breath hitched as I watched his incisor teeth sharpen and lengthen. I watched as if caught in a trance as he began to lean forward, his bloody gaze intent on my neck.

The sharp prick of his teeth as they ripped into my skin was the last thing I felt before I descended into blissful darkness.

1

RUNE

3 WEEKS EARLIER

Let me explain.

Daxon's words spun on my mind. All the while my wolf tore out of me viciously, the pain not comparing to the piercing ache of finding Rae tied to a table in the basement, his tongue cut out, and the man responsible... I choked on my breath at the thought.

Daxon had done this.

I shuddered as I lunged at him, white fur bristling across my skin, bones shifting. Teeth bared, I released a heavy growl.

I felt betrayed at what he did to Rae...I'd never known real love. And when I thought I finally had, he and Wilder ripped my heart to shreds. And now my head danced with untruths, with lies, with things I couldn't make sense of with my own eyes. I didn't want to believe Daxon was the killer in the woods. But if not, after what I'd just seen... What was he?

Maybe this was what finally destroyed me.

I slammed into him, my force propelling him backward. Inside my head, I was screaming.

He reeled, reacting too slowly, and he fell. He slammed to the floor onto his back, grunting, and I straddled his chest, glaring down at him.

"Rune," he snarled, his gaze narrowing on my wolf eyes.

My head was full of memories of us together... things my stupid heart refused to believe were lies. I couldn't live with that. Not after Wilder left me. Not when I had no idea how I'd take another breath if I lost them both. Not when I could never go back to them being anything but my lovers after I let them see into my soul?

Anger crashed through me, because nothing excused what Daxon had done. And nothing excused Wilder for leaving me for *her*.

Fury flared over me right through my bones, and I snapped down, my mouth biting into the meaty curve of Daxon's neck.

He bellowed, shoving a fist against my side, but it barely registered.

Blood seeped into my mouth--warm and so delicious. I slurped more of it, my teeth tearing deeper into his flesh, hitting bone.

I wanted him and Wilder to hurt, to cry like I had, to feel so trapped that their world would suffocate them.

My entire life, I'd been lied to, pushed aside, walked on. But the strength coursing through me was unlike anything I'd experienced before. My new strength made me brave, and I growled at the sensation, loving the power.

Daxon roared and shoved his hands into me, catching me unexpectedly.

I flew backward and hit the leg of the long, metal table, sending it rocking sideways. The entire thing crashed over behind me, with Rae still on it. Rae was growling with pain as he tumbled to his side.

I winced and drove myself back up, my heartbeat racing.

I sneered at Daxon as he got to his feet and towered over me.

In response, I peeled back my upper lip over my fangs so my threat was clear.

His chest puffed out, fists curled as blood from my bite rolled down his heaving chest like red ribbons.

"What the fuck are you doing, Rune! You're attacking me because of him?" He jutted an arm out toward Rae, who was now on the floor on the overturned table.

I growled in response with words he couldn't understand. The longer I stood in front of him, the more he got into my head.

When Rae's desperate pleas found me, rage took me over once again, and I leaped at Daxon.

His eyes widened at my attack, and he lunged out of the way, but he wasn't fast enough. Something about my wolf made me feel like I could fly. I left a trail of silver glitter behind me, just as I did every time I took wolf form.

I swung around incredibly fast, paws skidding across the floor, and came up behind Daxon before he could respond. Head first, I bowled into his back, sending him stumbling forward. Then I attacked, biting, ripping into him. We rolled on the floor, and I sensed nothing but the red fury pulsing within my veins.

He wrenched away from me in a sudden move and shoved himself up on his knees. Then he hurled himself on top of me so fast with an arm thrown around the back of my neck, putting me in a chokehold.

My head spun.

"Rune, fuck! I don't want to hurt you, but you've got to back the hell down."

Growling, I thrust against him, snapping, but he tightened his hold, and I gasped from a lack of oxygen. My back legs kicked out to find purchase, but I came up short.

When he released me, I stumbled out of his arms, coughing for breath to fill my lungs. A rumble escaped my throat, my wolf pushing to take me over completely, to show Daxon she was a worthy opponent. I could take him down!

"If you want to fight, then let's do it," he barked. "I won't back down, you know that, but you should also get your facts straight first. Then we can at least fight for the right reasons instead of over this piece of trash."

His words infuriated me, especially when to my side, Rae was writhing on the turned table, trying to free himself. I called my wolf back, and she slithered within me in seconds, skin replacing fur, bones stretching. Pulling up, I now stood in my human form once more, naked, while the taste of Daxon's blood coated the back of my throat.

I turned to face him.

"Please, Rune, it's not what it looks like. I mean, sure, I am going to kill Rae, even if he deserves so much worse."

"What are you doing, Daxon? You can't just kill who you want. What's wrong with you?"

He didn't scare me. I felt too broken, too hurt, and too far gone for fear. What I felt now, as the rage slipped away... was numb.

My pulse thundered in my ears with images of how devastated Miyu would be if she lost Rae. I recoiled back toward the table and glanced down at Rae who was shaking off the last of the restraints.

"Get up," I instructed. "We're getting out of here."

"You know I'm not going to let that happen," Daxon growled.

I took a panicked glance over my shoulder at him. But the words I wanted to say were stolen. Rae crashed into me so unexpectedly, I yelled. I hit the floor hard, all the breath driven from my lungs once more as his heavy body landed on top of mine.

And it all happened in a split second.

I frantically shoved against him, pushing my hands at his face, against his gaping mouth and snapping teeth. Shivers curled around my spine, and my heart was hammering in my chest. He violently bit my forearm as I shoved it between us.

Teeth tore my skin, sharp pain racing up my arm, and I bellowed. But when his eyes met mine, something else slid behind them. They didn't belong to Rae, but a predator.

He flew off me then, and Daxon hurled an arm around his throat, before kicking the back of his legs.

Rae fell to his knees while Daxon snatched a handful of his hair. "You see, Rune, our friend hasn't exactly been truthful with us. Have you?" He shook Rae's head forward, forcing him to nod.

Rae roared with a voice I barely recognized. It grew dark and gravelly, then he stared at me as if he looked through to my soul. "He's lying, Rune. Don't let him hurt me, please." His voice was garbled as he pleaded. The words hard to understand without his tongue. The hairs on my arms stood on end.

But the bite on my arm told a different story.

"Rae," I murmured, getting to my feet. "What have you done?"

I stared at the man who had married my best friend, who I thought I knew, but my head pulsed trying to make sense of it all. Blood and tears coated his face, he was a mess.

"What did he do?" I cradled my bitten arm to my chest, looking to Daxon for answers. Needing the truth.

"This asshole," Daxon snapped. "Has been preying on pack members for months now. He killed Eve, Mary, and Asher. He attacked his next victim near the woods today, but I caught him before he got the chance to butcher her."

My mouth hung open, and my mind blurred. No, this couldn't be real, yet pieces started to slip into place about how each body had been found near the woods. How recently I've noticed a dire change in Rae, who appeared despondent and distant. Miyu telling me he hadn't been himself. "B-but...this is Rae we're talking about. The guy who loves Miyu and tells bad jokes at the diner."

"And the devil doesn't appear with horns and a tail, but shows himself disguised as everything you'll trust," Daxon responded, quoting something I knew I had heard before somewhere.

"Why would you...?" I asked Rae, my voice cracking. "How could you do this to Miyu?"

His disposition darkened... I saw it in his shifting eyes, his curling posture. Then he lunged at me again, the hair in Daxon's fist ripped free.

I scrambled back, terror shuddering over me.

Daxon threw himself after Rae and wrenched him backward. Suddenly, Daxon was grasping a butcher's knife. Where the hell had that come from?

He yanked back Rae's head and sliced his throat in one quick swipe. The blade bit into flesh, blood pebbling instantly. Rae choked and blood spurted out, its warmth splattering my face.

I flinched and stumbled back until my heels hit the

wall. A cry pinched in my throat as Rae held my stare. I frantically wipe my face with my hand, needing his blood off me.

Daxon released him, and Rae hit the ground hard.

His muffled cries gurgled in his own blood. "Miyu..."

Then his head flopped to the side. He was gone.

"He's in a better place now," Daxon told me like it was supposed to ease the grief as he stepped over Rae, coming toward me.

Tears drenched my face, and I shook ferociously, a scream tearing from my throat.

Daxon collected me into his arms and lifted me off my feet. "It's going to be alright," he whispered soothingly while walking me upstairs and out of the basement. We ended up in the bathroom, and Daxon turned on the shower, steam quickly filling the room.

I sunk down on the cold floor, staring at the blood on my hands. I doubted anything would ever be alright again.

Rae was the killer. And Daxon had just murdered him.

"Let's wash you," he suggested.

I glanced up at Daxon, at him pulling off his boots and unbuckling his belt before dropping his pants, then standing completely naked in front of me. This powerful man was dangerous.

"I don't understand. Why would he kill anyone?" My voice quivered, and I blinked hard to keep the tears away.

He shook his head. "I don't know, sweetheart. I asked him, trust me, but it was like something had snapped inside him. He wasn't himself. I've never seen him this way before, but I know what I saw him do near the woods with my own eyes. And I ended his killing spree."

I sniffled as he took my hands and lifted me to my feet. "It doesn't make sense," I said as he wrapped his arms around me and guided me to the shower. "We should have smelled his scent on the murder scenes, but no one did."

Doubt thrummed through me that this was a horrible mistake, that it couldn't have been Rae.

I stood in front of Daxon, both of us naked, and his hand on my back as he nudged me under the water. I couldn't stop the tears. Because I knew the truth... Rae had in fact killed those people even if I wanted it to not be real.

This would ruin Miyu.

"What I saw in the woods earlier matched all the other killings. He attacked a young girl from behind and knocked her out. What he didn't know was that I surveyed the woods today, watching, waiting. And I found him. He won't be killing anyone else ever again." His voice grew low despite the awful encounter. "I can't explain why his scent wasn't at the other murders, but I will find out."

Hot water cascaded over my head and body, bringing with it an awakening.

He cupped my face, standing in the shower with me, blood streaming down his chest from my bite, from Rae's death. The attack on my arm hurt as the water splashed over it.

"His loss hurts now, but he won't harm another person." He lifted my arm and gently cleaned Rae's bite mark. "You'll heal in no time. It doesn't look deep."

It was already getting better standing there, or maybe that was just because my entire body was going numb.

Daxon collected the soap and rolled it between his hands, creating frothing suds.

"I know that," I muttered. "It's that I thought I knew him, but I was wrong. I mean, look at Wilder. What else in this town is a lie?" I choked on the words and squeezed my eyes shut, lifting my head into the water to chase away the ugly cry that twisted in my chest.

"I saw Wilder in the woods tonight. He was kissing Daria," I admitted to Daxon and he stiffened at my words.

"Fuck, baby," he responded, rubbing my back comfortingly.

I wished more than anything for Wilder to be here, to be the man I had hoped he was. But I wasn't enough for him, or he wouldn't have left me.

Behind my clenched eyes, Rae's face flashed and his last word echoed in my ears. *Miyu.*

I hiccuped a breath. A feeling of dread and uncertainty came over me.

I missed Wilder. Missed Rae. Wished Daxon hadn't killed him.

Daxon ran a gentle touch over my neck, and I opened my eyes as he wiped the blood from my shoulder and face. He quickly rinsed the suds away from my wound with clear water, and he tended to me gently, lingering a bit too long on cupping my breasts.

A spark rose through me, breaking through the emptiness that had swallowed me.

He watched me carefully. "You're so beautiful, and I hate it when you cry. I would destroy the world if it brought back your smile."

I pressed my body to his, something about his words filling me with a desperate need to feel him all over me. "Please, tell me again that everything is going to be alright."

His expression soothed, and he responded softly, "Okay, sweetheart. I'll make sure everything is okay soon. I promise you."

Suddenly, he kissed me, our mouths clashing like our souls were merging, and I didn't know how much I needed him until now. I was a lost girl in the arms of a man who killed murderers, and it should terrify me. It did, but I was so torn and broken from unbearable grief, with a need to stop hurting, that he was exactly what I craved at that moment.

I breathed against his mouth. "Make me feel anything but this horrible pain. I feel like it's breaking me apart." Maybe I was a coward or it was selfish of me that I wanted to avoid the inevitable reality that Rae was dead, that Miyu would be devastated, and that nothing would be the same again.

Daxon's eyes lit up, the feral appearance in them belonging to a man who wanted me more than air to breathe.

That single look broke down my walls, and I kissed him back just as hard, just as fast, just as demanding.

A strong arm looped around my middle as his other hand grabbed my nape. There was urgency in the way he pinned me to the wall and plunged his tongue into my mouth, tasting all of me. My hands tangled in his hair, and I moaned at the way he claimed me completely.

Daxon had never been a man with patience or taking his time when it came to me. He was rough, leaving a trail of hot kisses on my neck, taking mock bites.

"You belong to me," he growled in my ear.

I almost forgot how to breathe. But instead of claiming me, he lifted my chin and kissed me, softer this time. Like he'd come to the realization that I was so brittle emotionally, that he might devastate me further.

Hot water sprayed us, and I bathed in the protectiveness he was offering me.

"You smell so delicious, baby," he groaned and took another deep inhale against my neck. "But I'm not going to fuck you today, Rune. I'm going to wash you, then hold you for as long as you need."

A blaze flared behind his hazel eyes. He was irresistible, but I knew sex wasn't going to fix me tonight, and my tears began once again. They streamed down my cheeks, and he kissed me all over my face.

Electricity hummed over my skin at his touch.

He collected the soap and moved to wash my stomach, kneeling in front of me as if he might worship me.

Admittedly, what he said earlier wasn't what he wanted, but it made me realize how much he tried to change for me. To show me the gentler side of him instead of the wolf in the night others feared.

But in my mind, I couldn't stop seeing Rae on the floor in a pool of his blood, his throat sliced, and his wife's name on his lips.

Tears kept falling.

The way Daxon eliminated him so swiftly, without remorse, worried me. Everything had happened so quickly, the shock still in my body, but the more I thought about what happened, the more a different kind of fear climbed through me.

If Rae lost his mind and became so feral that he killed others, how different was he to Daxon? Did he believe by punishing those deserving of death, he was vindicated?

I suppressed a shudder and asked, "I feel sick to my stomach for Miyu. Do you feel anything after killing Rae?"

He lifted his head to meet my gaze. "What can I say that won't upset you?"

"The truth." Heat burned across my chest. I had to know the truth, to hear it from his lips. I dragged myself away from him, pressing into the corner of the shower.

He stood up, and I was so tiny compared to him, but I held my chin high. "I have to know who you really are."

Miyu... Rae's voice rang inside my head.

He sighed and shook his head as if disappointed, then placed the soap back into the ceramic holder on the wall. A trail of blood welled from the bite on his neck, and it slipped down his chest.

"Yes, I feel remorse for the pain this is going to bring Miyu. I've lost a friend too, a Bitten pack member. Those things I grieve about. But do I regret killing him? Not after what he did."

My stomach tangled at his response. He was just killing in the name of justice, right? But what if there had been a chance to save Rae? We didn't exactly know what was wrong with him yet. So what if we could have saved him?

I knew I should ask if this was something Daxon did often, what with the whole secret torture room under his house...but I couldn't bring myself to face that quite yet.

Maybe I was a coward.

Bile rose in the back of my throat. I was going to be sick if I kept thinking that way. But I couldn't shake the thoughts away. For all I knew, Rae had always been this way, always killing but only recently became more brazen.

Everything was happening so fast. My heart raced. While the room tilted around me. I had enough chaos in my world, enough death, and yet it seemed to gravitate toward me.

Miyu...

Moments earlier, I was in a state of shock, and I'd been craving Daxon's kiss. Now, those warm-hearted feelings faded away, replaced with something else. Something dark.

I wanted to be as far from him as possible. To work out what the hell I was going to do... and to pay Miyu a visit.

I dreaded our conversation, but she'd find out eventually. And it was better if it came from me.

"Rune," Daxon placated. "Everything will be okay."

"No, no it won't," I snapped. Anger and heartbreak carved a path right into my soul. Images of Rae dead sped through my mind, blending into my emotions with the urgency of my beating pulse.

I pushed past Daxon desperately, shoving the glass door to the shower aside. "I need to go. I can't stay here..." My voice broke off and I ran out of the bathroom.

2

RUNE

Disgust. It coated my skin, enveloping all of my senses as I walked towards town. How had my life managed to fall apart like this in such a short amount of time? I thought I was past the darkness and finally heading towards my happily ever after.

I never imagined something like this.

The image of Rae lying there on the table assaulted my brain, so swift and sudden that I had to stop and puke at the side of the path. I could hear shuffling from nearby, and I turned my head, my senses on alert, only to see that it was a worried looking Daxon, apparently following me.

I didn't bother telling him to go away. Daxon would do what he wanted. He and Wilder both would. Obviously.

Wilder. Even with what had just happened, just his name shredded my insides. That kiss. It echoed in my mind even as a nasty voice inside of me asked me what I'd expected. Hadn't I wanted Wilder and Daxon? Why couldn't he have done the same?

I shuddered, and bile rose up in my throat again.

Get yourself together, I snapped at myself, before

straightening and heading back to town, steadfastly ignoring Daxon who continued to follow me.

How did I get myself in this situation over and over again? How did I continue to let myself destroy me over and over?

It was no one's fault but my own. Instead of running right into the arms of a man...instead of trusting my heart with a man... I should have worked on myself. I was the only one that I could trust not to shatter me into a million pieces.

At least that was what I was trying to tell myself. I had a feeling that no matter what I tried to say, it wouldn't be able to erase the unending ache that I'd had since I'd seen Wilder locked together with *her.*

It all went back to my thoughts on that long drive to this town in the first place. Maybe I was destined to live a miserable life forever and ever.

And it would be all my fault.

I got to the main street of the town, stuck in my self-pity cycle, and almost immediately heard the familiar sound of Miyu laughing. I looked down the sidewalk and saw her standing next to a dapper-looking Mr. Jones. She threw her head back and laughed again, and I hadn't thought it was possible, since I couldn't exactly remember the last time that I ate, but I bent over and threw up again.

"Rune!" Miyu called out worriedly, and I heard the sound of her footsteps running towards me until I got the courage to stand up and face her. "Are you sick? Do you need me to take you to the doctor?" she asked. Her face was drawn and tired, nights of worrying about Rae catching up to her.

They were about to get a whole lot worse.

A throat cleared nearby, and I looked behind me to see that Daxon was almost to us.

I realized that I had no idea what to say. Did I tell her that Daxon had killed her mate? Did I tell her that the person she had bound her life to was the one who had been slaughtering members of this pack? For a second, Eve's lifeless gaze filled my memory, and I wondered if I was forever doomed to be haunted by the dead.

I was not prepared for this. I opened my mouth and then closed it again.

"What is it?" Miyu asked in a rattled voice, tears filling her eyes as if she was already prepared for the worst.

"I'm sorry, Miyu. Rae's dead," Daxon said, his voice a perfect mixture of horror and sadness. It hit me then how effortlessly he had managed to flit around this pack this whole time, convincing them he was someone he definitely wasn't.

Miyu froze, her skin paling as she absorbed what Daxon had just said. She shook her head as if in a daze.

"I'm sorry, what did you just say?" she asked, the words coming out in a whisper.

"Miyu, I'm so sorry," I said to her in a tear-stricken voice. Her body was trembling, and I watched in horror as the words finally sank in. I saw the light in Miyu's eyes completely disappear like a flame extinguishing in the night. She wrapped her arms around herself, tears beginning to streak down her face.

"I don't understand. I—I just saw him this morning. We had breakfast, and he kissed me goodbye...and now you're saying he's just gone?" A hitched sob tore out of her. "Can someone fucking tell me what is going on," she screamed, her words echoing down the sidewalk and beginning to draw a crowd.

I stepped towards her, wanting to throw my arms around her even if I was the last person who should be offering her any comfort.

She stumbled backward like I'd come at her with a knife. "Don't touch me!" she shrieked. There was a wildness to her gaze as she looked around, as though Rae was about to appear from behind a building at any moment.

In a lifetime of heartbreak, watching Miyu fall apart was one of the worst things that I'd ever seen.

I pulled at my shirt helplessly, not knowing what to do, or what to say.

"Can we talk somewhere privately?" Daxon asked, looking around at the anxious crowd that was gathering around us.

Miyu pulled at the bottom of her long hair before frantically brushing it out of her face. "Okay," she whimpered, and she allowed me to take her arm and lead her down the street. There was an office building a block away that Wilder and Daxon both used occasionally for town business. Daxon led the way towards that.

Miyu looked at me as I practically hauled her down the street. She was putting almost all of her weight on me as we walked, sobs wracking through her body. "Tell me this is just a dream," she whimpered, gazing at me desperately.

I was crying too—silent, guilty tears that I felt ashamed to allow. "I wish I could, sweetheart," I murmured, and her cries grew louder.

The walk to the office building might as well have been ten miles for how long it felt to get there. People stared curiously at us as we walked by, their interest turning to fear as they saw Miyu crying. Miyu was emotional. There was rarely a time that she wasn't bursting with emotion, whether it was happiness or anger, or excitement. But I doubt many of them had ever seen her cry.

Daxon unlocked the front glass door and walked inside, the two of us following him closely. He locked the door after us and drew down the blinds so that nosy bystanders couldn't see in.

I led Miyu over to a chair and gently sat her down before settling in next to her. Daxon pulled over a chair and sat down across from us. It was dim and gloomy, the cloudiness of the day seeping in and blanketing everything.

"Miyu, this is going to be difficult to hear," Daxon began as I took Miyu's hand.

My stomach twisted in knots in anticipation of what he was about to say. Vibrant red blood cut across my vision. Rae's screams echoed in my ears as flashbacks splashed through my mind.

Get yourself fucking together, I told myself sternly. *This isn't about you.*

"Rae was responsible for all the recent town killings," he said calmly.

There was silence for a long moment. Miyu was holding onto my hand for dear life, and I was afraid she was going to break the bones in my hand with how tight her grip was.

Suddenly, she pulled her hand away and sprang from her seat. "Is this some kind of sick joke?" she screeched. "What the hell is wrong with you people?" Her eyes sliced down at me, betrayal thick in her gaze.

"Miyu, he's telling you the truth," I told her brokenly.

She scoffed. "Rae takes bugs outside instead of killing them! He once kept a rabid squirrel with a broken leg in our house for a month because he "wanted to help it." That damn squirrel literally ate holes in half of my shoes while I was gone one day. Rae is not the killer."

A red flush mottled her usually perfect skin, and her breath was coming out in gasps. Her lips were trembling as she tried to convince us...or herself, that we were wrong.

"Has Rae been disappearing lately? Has he had mood swings? Have you felt like he was hiding something from you?" Daxon pressed calmly.

His face was the picture of concern, but I wondered, staring at him, if he actually felt any sorrow for the news he was delivering...that he was the one who was responsible for it. It was hard to comprehend how he could claim he loved me, that he was obsessed with me, but have no emotion for anything else.

Miyu's hitched gasp pulled my attention away as her face somehow blanched, becoming even more pale, and she sank back down in her seat. Her hands were balled into fists, and she brought them up in front of her quivering mouth as if she could somehow block everything out around her.

"People get stressed," she whispered. "That's all it was. It was just stress."

Daxon bent over and grabbed a large black bag from the floor that I had somehow missed him carrying around.

He reached into the bag and pulled out several chunks of hair in various colors. There was blood streaked across most of them. I shivered when I realized what it was.

"I found this in Rae's car, Miyu," he said sympathetically. "He was keeping trophies of his victims. I even found a bag of blood-stained clothes in his trunk that he hadn't had a chance to get rid of. He was the killer."

Right there in that chair, in that small office that had seen better days, I watched Miyu's soul die. The sound that came out of her mouth was something that I knew would haunt my dreams. Her pain was tangible in the air; you could taste it, feel it beating against your skin.

She was broken.

"Get her back to her house, Rune," Daxon directed as he stood up, placing the hair back in the bag. For a second, I wondered if he took trinkets from his victims too, and the urge to throw up hit me again. I couldn't look at him.

"Come on," I said softly as I put my arm around her. I led her out of the office, then onto the sidewalk where, luckily, the crowd had dispersed.

"Rune," Daxon growled to our backs. I sighed and shot him a quick glance even as I kept walking, unable to hide the multitude of confusion, disgust, sadness...and fear I was experiencing. "I'll give you tonight, but I won't give you forever. There isn't a story that doesn't end with us, even if you don't believe it right now."

The words wrapped around my tattered heart like a golden thread that warmed my insides...even when they shouldn't.

I was a broken girl, holding my broken friend, and I wondered at that moment if I deserved every single bad thing that's ever happened to me.

I didn't answer him. I just continued to stagger away, holding up most of Miyu's weight as she continued to fall apart. I doubted she even heard him through the depths of her tears and sorrow.

But I couldn't breathe until we turned the corner and I was away from his gaze.

We stumbled our way to Miyu's house, the one that she and Rae had just bought right before their mating ceremony.

We paused on the front steps, and she stared unblinkingly at the door.

"Where's your key?" I asked her gently, and she dug around in her pocket for a moment before handing it to me without a word.

I braced myself as I turned the key in the lock and got the door open, because Rae was everywhere...

As he should be in this place. But I had two versions of Rae in my head, and neither fit with what I saw as I led her down the hallway littered with pictures of them together, to the living room that had his flannel draped on one of the chairs.

His boots were in the corner, and their beers from last night were still sitting on the coffee table. Above the fireplace was a huge canvas from their ceremony...before I disappeared, obviously. They were kissing, so much joy written on their faces that it made me physically ache.

I half expected him to come around the corner to scoop Miyu up and kiss her tears away. I didn't know that a house could become haunted in just a few hours.

But this one already was.

I set Miyu down on the couch and ran into the kitchen where I grabbed a glass and filled it with water. I rushed back to the living room and handed it to her, but the glass slipped out of her hand and fell to the ground, the water seeping out onto the thick cream carpet that I knew Rae had just installed. They'd bought a fixer-upper and were in the process of remodeling it. The carpet had just gone in last week.

Miyu looked up at me, desperation seeping out of her. "What am I supposed to do? Where's his body? How did he die? And the funeral, do I still hold it?" The words rushed out of her, and I didn't know what to say. I couldn't tell her *how* Rae died.

"He was trying to run away when he was caught, and

there was an accident," I finally told her haltingly, not understanding why I felt this need to protect Daxon and keep the truth of what he'd done a secret.

For all I knew, Daxon was just as dangerous as Rae had been.

But he's ours, my wolf growled.

Shut up, I responded crossly back to her.

An aching moan came out of Miyu, breaking me out of my inner arguments with my wolf.

"His body will be taken care of, and we can worry about everything else tomorrow, I think," I rushed out, tentatively stroking her back in an attempt to comfort her even though I felt like the villain in her story right now. "Should I call your aunt to be with you tonight?"

She nodded numbly and handed me her cell phone. I quickly found her aunt's contact information and called her. After explaining the situation as quickly as I could, her aunt frantically assured me she'd be right over, and we hung up.

The silence of the room felt deafening. Miyu wasn't crying anymore. Hell, she was barely breathing. She just sat there staring at the wall in front of her.

Miyu stood abruptly, making me jump, and she practically ran down the hallway to where I knew their bedroom was. I followed her tentatively and saw her sitting on her bed holding a pillow to her chest as tears once again streamed down her face.

"His smell is going to fade," she sobbed as she pulled the pillow up to her face. "Then what am I going to do?" Her sobs started to become hysterical. "This is just a dream," she started to chant over and over again.

I stayed in the doorway, not knowing what to do. She looked how I felt at the moment. Even though my loves were both alive, it felt like I'd lost them in a permanent way that seemed soul-destroying.

"Oh, honey," I heard a voice say, and I moved aside as a plump older woman with dark brown hair liberally streaked with gray pushed past me and went to Miyu's side.

It must be her aunt.

Miyu's sobs increased as she threw herself into the woman's arms, and I slowly backed out of the room, feeling like an intruder. Not just because of her aunt, but because Rae's scent was everywhere, stronger in their room than anywhere else.

It was devastating.

I stayed in the living room for thirty minutes, listening as Miyu's sobs echoed throughout the house. They finally died, and a few minutes later, the woman came out to where I was sitting.

"She's finally asleep, poor dear," she said quietly, wringing her hands in distress. "You'd better go on home too. I'll stay with her until she decides she wants me gone."

"Okay," I answered tiredly, standing up. "I'm Rune, by the way."

"I don't think there is anyone in this town that doesn't know you, dear," she said with a sad smile. "It's nice to meet you, even in such unfortunate circumstances. My niece has talked very fondly about you. I'm Alicia."

She sighed, and a tear fell down her cheek. "Get some sleep. We're all going to need it."

I nodded and walked towards the door, taking one look back only to see Alicia weeping as she sat down in a chair.

After I exited the house, I stood on the front porch for a long moment, realizing that I wasn't sure where to go. I'd been staying with Wilder and Daxon. I'd thought that I'd found my home.

And now I knew I was wrong.

I set off down the path that led back into the main thoroughfare, a shiver still passing over my skin as I looked at the thick woods to the left of me. I came to a screeching halt when I saw a large, shadowed figure watching me from just within the treeline.

What the hell was that? I began to sprint towards town, and I swear whoever it was, was taunting me, keeping pace with me but staying in the treeline so I couldn't see it clearly.

But Rae was dead though, I'd seen it for myself. Was this just some asshole playing a trick? Had Daxon been wrong? Was the killer somewhere out there?

I kept on sprinting, my breath coming out in gasps. I looked over to the woods again and screamed when I saw the same creature that I'd seen on the day Eve had died step out and grin at me.

"Rune," Daxon yelled, and suddenly I was in his arms. "What's wrong?"

"The—the creature was there. The killer isn't dead. He's still out there. You killed the wrong person," I sobbed as I began to beat on his chest.

Daxon gently grabbed my fists and held them still against his chest, peering into the woods over my shoulder. I shot a panicked look behind me, my breath stilling for a moment when I realized that whatever I'd seen had disappeared.

For a second, I doubted myself.

Had I just imagined it? Had the stress of the last few days...scratch that, my entire life, finally pushed me over the edge and broke my hold on reality?

But it seemed so real.

"I swear to you, Rae was the killer. Whatever you saw

was something else," Daxon said soothingly, obviously having the same suspicion that I was currently experiencing, that I'd just imagined it.

His tone made me irrationally angry.

"I'm not imagining it," I scoffed, not exactly sure which of us I was angry at. I pushed away from him and stalked back towards town. But not too fast...I didn't want to get eaten, after all.

"Rune, wait," he sighed exasperatedly as he quickly caught up with me. "Where exactly are you going? Where's Miyu?"

I stopped and twirled around. "That's the whole problem, isn't it? I have no idea where I'm going, and Miyu is currently asleep, probably cuddling her dead mate's pillow after she hysterically cried for hours."

Daxon's face flickered with pain. I didn't know whether he was actually feeling pain or just faking it. I didn't know anything.

How was it possible that my world had changed so dramatically, so fast?

I suddenly felt exhausted, and my shoulders drooped. "I'm just going to go to the inn tonight, Daxon. We can talk about everything tomorrow."

Daxon pushed a hand through his hair, clearly exasperated with me, but didn't object as I pushed farther away from him and strode back onto Main Street.

News of Rae's death clearly hadn't spread because the town was alive with people. I realized it was Friday night.

I passed one of the cafes and came to a screeching halt when I saw him. Wilder. He was sitting at a table.

With Daria.

It felt like death by a thousand cuts at that moment. As if the day couldn't get any worse. I could swear that someone was stabbing me with a hot poker as I watched her trail her crimson red-painted fingernail down the side of his face. And then he smiled at her, like she was everything. Like how he used to smile at me.

My hands wrapped around my waist. Was I bleeding? It felt like all of my insides had to be seeping out of me.

When he leaned towards her, and I knew their lips were about to touch, I sprinted away, wishing that I were dead.

I had only taken a few steps when I smacked right into a firm chest, almost crumpling to the ground upon impact before I was caught by a strong pair of arms.

My head snapped up, only to be snared by a captivating pair of blue eyes the color of a cloudless night sky at midnight.

"Whoa there, pretty girl. You alright?"

He looked blurry through my tear-streaked eyes, but even though I was a mess, I couldn't help but notice...he was gorgeous. His hair was dark and streaked with a blue color that almost matched his eyes, with slight curls here and there. His face belonged to a fallen angel, each feature perfectly symmetrical. Straight dark eyebrows over those strikingly dark eyes. A mouth that was begging to be...

Okay, that was a weird thought.

The most important trait about the man currently holding me in his arms like I was precious, staring down at me as if I was the most fascinating thing he'd ever seen, was that he was a stranger. I haven't seen him before.

And strangers didn't come to Amarok.

"Excuse me," I murmured, my tears coming to an abrupt halt as my wolf perked up inside of me, sensing danger.

Was this some kind of hunter?

I tried to surreptitiously sniff the air, wondering if I

could figure out if he was a wolf, but I wasn't getting anything.

"You're welcome to run into me anytime," he said with a pretty grin that made something flutter inside of me.

I laughed awkwardly before inelegantly moving out of his grasp. I pushed a piece of hair out of my face, wishing I had a rock to hide under so that I didn't have to see anyone.

"I'm Ares," he said, holding out his hand to shake even though I'd literally been in his arms just a second ago. I tentatively shook it, half expecting Daxon to pop out of the alley at any moment and cut off the guy's head.

But I didn't see him amid the crowd.

Just then, I heard Wilder's laugh coming from somewhere behind me, and blind panic flashed through me.

"Welcome to town," I said quickly, pushing past him in desperation to disappear before Wilder saw me.

"I'll see you around?" Ares called after me, and I waved my hand behind my back, single-mindedly focused on getting to the inn as fast as I could.

I burst through the door of the inn, running right into the crowded bar area. Jim was cleaning glasses behind the bar and saw me right away. He put the glass down and popped his head into the back room where the kitchen was. A moment later, Carrie came hustling out, coming right towards me.

"Hi, darling. What are you doing here?" she asked, putting her arm around me and leading me towards the stairs that led to the rooms.

"Just taking a break," I murmured.

"Okay," she said understandingly. "Old Mr. Hubbard is staying in your old room tonight. His wife kicked him out again for getting drunk at the bar last night. But the room at the end of the hall that has that nice view of the river is open." Carrie handed me a key with a soft smile.

"Thank you," I said, squeezing her arm before trudging up the familiar steps, walking down the hall, and sticking the key into the lock. It opened with a soft click into a room that looked pretty much identical to the room I'd first stayed in. I closed the door and locked it behind me, leaning against the door, not knowing if I wanted to cry or scream or fall to the ground in exhaustion.

It felt different though. There had been an air of possibility when I'd been in the other room. I'd had quite a few lows, but there was still the feeling that something was going to happen, that things were on the verge of being great. When I stayed in that room, I'd had Wilder and Daxon.

And now I had neither.

A knock sounded on the door just then, and I flinched. "Who is it?" I called softly, not having the energy to deal with anything else tonight.

"Let me in, Rune," Daxon murmured through the door. My wolf settled inside of me at the sound of his voice, even if the rest of me wanted to throw something.

"I need some space, Daxon. I thought I made that clear."

"Rune, if you would just talk to me, tell me what's going on in your head, tell me how I can fix this."

What if it can't be fixed?

The thought flashed through my head and I pushed it away. That couldn't be the reality. But even as I thought that, Wilder's face glued to that fae wench pushed through, and then Miyu's tear-stained face followed that.

"Please," I said through the door, not even sure what I was asking for at this point.

"I'm not leaving, Rune," Daxon growled, and I heard a thump and then some movement before realizing that he had slid to the ground and was leaning against the door.

I slid to the ground too, absurdly finding comfort that he was just on the other side of the door. The moon shone in from the window across from me, and I stared at it like the lovesick moron I was, wondering if Wilder was looking at the same one and maybe thinking of me.

And with that thought, I fell into a troubled, restless sleep.

3
RUNE

I stood up and opened the door. Daxon was slumped over, his soft snores echoing down the hallway. I walked past him and down the stairs through the now empty lobby and bar, and then I walked outside into the quiet streets. I walked on and on until...

I screamed as I woke up and found myself in a pitch-black room. Trembling, I looked around, trying to figure out where I was. How had I gotten here? Had I walked in my sleep again?

I felt a tiny moment of relief when I realized where I was. The town hall.

Not that it was particularly heartwarming during the day, but it was definitely a bit scary at night. The small bits of lights coming through the dusty windows cast strange shadows over everything, and I jumped when something skittered nearby.

Please tell me that it was just a rat.

I walked over to the huge double doors and pulled on them, only to find out that they were locked and I had no idea how to unlock them. How the hell had I gotten into this place if not through those doors?

Goosebumps prickled across my skin as I gave up on the doors and stared around the room, looking for any other ways to get out. My footsteps might as well have been bombs with how loud they sounded as I walked in between the chairs, looking for any doors. When I got to the front of the room where Daxon and Wilder usually stood for meetings, I screeched as something loud thumped from the shadows.

"Hello?" I called out, my voice trembling. This was bad. This was very bad. My thoughts jumped to the monster in the woods. Had it followed me in here? My imagination was running wild.

I realized suddenly that the air had become freezing. My breath was coming out in puffs of vapor.

I had to get out of here.

Out of the corner of my eye, a light caught my attention, and I screamed again when I looked to my left and I saw a form walking towards me, a soft light shining around them as if they were backlit.

Being the graceful creature that I was, I stumbled backward and fell to the floor in my effort to get away. I tried to keep scooting backward in my desperation but found myself hitting the wall. My wolf was pointedly not coming to my aid, not that I thought she would have some sort of super power against whatever this thing was still approaching me, but I wouldn't have minded her handling it for me.

As the light came closer, I could see that it was a young girl, or that she used to be a young girl. She was definitely a spirit now. She gave off a different energy than Arcadia had though, and obviously looked far more ghostly than

Arcadia had since I hadn't even known Arcadia was dead until later. With Arcadia though, I could feel she wanted to harm me. Somehow, I knew that this ghost meant no harm.

She stopped walking when she was just a few feet away and watched me sadly.

"Can you hear me?" I asked, thinking of Arcadia and everything she'd been able to do in her ghostly form.

She nodded.

Before I could say anything else, another ghostly form emerged from a wall, this one a man in a colonial-style outfit that looked like he'd just stepped off the dance floor with George Washington himself.

"He's coming. He asked that you wait for him," the man said in a whispery voice that brushed against my skin like a frosty breeze.

"Who's coming?" I asked, thinking that there were probably a lot of dead people that I did not want to meet.

The ghost didn't answer, and I realized that I of course knew who was coming.

Rae.

For a second, I considered running away. My last inter-action with him had been him trying to kill me. Would he try and murder me again like Arcadia had?

I scrambled to my feet, but the young girl held up her hands pleadingly. "Please," she mouthed.

"Why can't I hear you?" I asked dumbly...since she obvi-ously couldn't respond to tell me.

"She was mute in her life," the other spirit answered for her.

"Oh," I said, wringing my hands together, wondering how I managed to be awkward even with ghosts.

But all thoughts of being awkward disappeared when, a second later, he appeared.

Rae.

He came through the doors that I hadn't been able to get to open, and he stood there for a long moment, just staring at me.

My whole body tensed, ready for him to all of a sudden pounce and try and finish me off. But after a long minute of the two of us just standing there, I realized that the manic, off energy he'd been exuding for weeks was completely gone.

He was just Rae, the man who had befriended me in the diner almost as soon as I arrived.

That somehow made the situation all the more devastating.

Belatedly, I realized that the other two spirits had disappeared, leaving just me and him.

"Hi," he said softly, taking a few tentative steps towards me as if he was afraid to scare me.

"Don't come any closer," I called out, as if I could control a ghost.

Was this some kind of trick? Was he trying to lure me into a false sense of security before attacking?

"How is she?" he responded as he stopped moving.

My insides curdled as I thought about Miyu, about how she'd been destroyed.

"How do you think she is? She just lost the fucking love of her life because you turned out to be a psycho," I spit the words out, even knowing how irrational it was to be yelling at a ghost. Not to mention how dangerous it was based on his homicidal tendencies while living.

All my anger seeped out when I saw him sink to his knees, a picture of devastation.

"I just need you to tell her I love her, and that I'll love her forever. There won't be a day that passes that she won't be all I think about...." He covered his face for a long moment as sobs wracked through his body.

I didn't know what to think as I stared at the ghost falling apart in front of me.

What did it say about love, that it was so powerful we had to carry the weight of it even into the afterlife? That was all well and good if you and your love skipped off into the sunset together, but what about the broken love stories that most of us experienced? The love stories that tore at our souls and we wished we could just forget?

Whoever wrote that it was better to have loved and lost than never to have loved at all could go fuck themselves because they clearly had never been in love.

I would give anything to not love anyone right now.

"Do you think she'll ever forgive me?" Rae asked, breaking me out of my brutal tirade against love.

"Do you deserve forgiveness?" I responded quietly, still very confused about the Rae I was experiencing right now. As I peered closer at him, I realized that he was fainter than he had been when he first appeared.

He looked confused by my question. His forehead wrinkled, like he was thinking hard about something he just couldn't grasp.

"I just can't remember when it all started. I don't understand why it started." He put his hands through his hair and pulled on the roots in frustration.

Suddenly, he lunged forward, traveling the whole room in a second until he was just inches away from me.

I was plastered against the wall, unable to go anywhere else.

"My notebook. Tell her to check my notebook," he muttered nonsensically before disappearing into thin air.

I froze for a second, the silence deafening after everything I'd just experienced.

There were so many questions whirling through my head. But I would think about those later. For now, I needed to figure out how to get the fuck out of here before any more ghosts appeared. I'd had enough.

I found a hallway off to the side, and I ran down it until I found an exit at the end.

I burst out into the cool night air, relief flooding over me that I'd made it out.

How the fuck had I gotten in there to begin with? Sleepwalking was a freaky thing.

My wolf surged forward, forcing the shift for the first time. I didn't fight her. The events of the last few days were crashing over me, and it felt good for a second to just let her take the reins.

We raced forward, the ground wet and cool under our paws, our silvery footsteps leaving a path behind us.

She had no fear as she ran towards the river. She didn't care about monsters or killers, rejected mates, or all the other boogie monsters that had haunted me lately. My wolf slowed as she reached the river's edge. She stretched out under the moon, shaking her fur out as she drank some of the water.

I was tempted to stay in this form forever, to never have to face all the problems waiting for me. But Rae's words echoed in my head.

"My notebook. Tell her to check my notebook."

It was the middle of the night, and I knew Miyu needed sleep, but I had to tell her what had just happened. I pushed my wolf to run towards Miyu's house, and she reluctantly allowed the shift once we got to Miyu's front steps. Something wet slid from my nose, and I frowned as I wiped at it and realized that my nose was bleeding. Must be all the stress. I could see through the front window that her aunt was curled up on the couch, and I debated whether or not to knock.

But I would want to know. She would probably want to go back to the town hall and try to talk to him again. A shiver passed over me just thinking about it. I'd do it for her though.

I softly tapped on the window, and her aunt woke with a start, springing up to a sitting position and looking around. She spotted me through the window and frowned before getting up and walking over to the door to let me in.

"Rune, I thought you were going to come back in the morning."

I shifted nervously, feeling foolish that I'd felt such a rush to get over here.

"My notebook."

"I need to talk to Miyu."

She looked behind her at the clock ticking on the wall. I flinched when I saw that it was four A.M. This was truly the night that would never end.

Alicia sighed and grabbed a robe that was hanging on a hook by the door. She handed it to me since I had no clothes on from my shift.

I'd forgotten about that little detail. I grabbed the robe and quickly pulled it on.

"I'm not sure—" she began, but I was already walking back towards Miyu's room. Her footsteps sounded behind me, but she stopped when she saw I was already standing in the doorway of Miyu's room. I looked in, painfully sighing at the sight of Miyu sound asleep, curled up with the pillow from Rae's side of the bed.

I took a few steps in, and she must have been sleeping

restlessly because her eyes popped open and she stared at me sadly, not looking at all surprised to see me there. "Tell me it was just a dream," she murmured, a tear slipping down her cheek.

I walked over to the bed and crawled in beside her, and she cuddled up next to me. "I saw Rae tonight after I sleep-walked to the town hall," I blurted out.

Miyu didn't even move at the news.

"His ghost," she said softly, still not sounding phased. I lifted my head up to look at her, but she was just staring at the ceiling, teardrops still tracking down her face.

I realized she was in shock; she wasn't absorbing anything that I was saying. I would have to tell her as soon as she came back to me.

"I'll get you through this," I told her, even though her eyes were closing.

"Stay," she whispered, holding onto my hand as she slipped into sleep once again.

"I promise," I whispered back. I stared up at the ceiling until I could see the faint rays of morning through the blinds...and then I finally fell asleep.

———

"Rune!" Daxon's voice yelled, rousing me from my fitful sleep. My eyes opened, and it took me a second to realize where I was. Miyu's house. I'd come back after...I'd seen Rae's freaking ghost!

The notebook!

I sat up right as Daxon frantically crashed through the door to Miyu's room, followed by a frazzled-looking Alicia. Her hair was sticking up all over the place, and she was carrying a broom that she looked to be seconds away from hitting Daxon upside the head with.

Daxon's frame immediately relaxed when he saw me, and he strode over the bed and grabbed me out of it. I squeaked as he hugged me like he hadn't seen me for years. "I fell asleep and you were gone."

I couldn't help but hug him back, allowing myself to bask in his familiar scent for one long moment before forcing myself to pull away. "I sleepwalked," I admitted. "It's a long story."

"You saw Rae," Miyu suddenly yelped, and I looked over to see her struggling to get out from under the blankets she'd wrapped around herself during the night.

"You saw Rae?" Daxon asked incredulously.

Daxon reluctantly set me down, and I took a step back so I could look at both of them. "When I sleepwalked to the town hall...there were ghosts," I began, knowing how crazy I sounded. "And Rae appeared." I focused on Miyu. "He told me to tell you that he would always love you. And he talked about a...notebook?"

"A notebook?" Miyu murmured, frowning as she gazed at me.

"He said to tell you to look at a notebook," I said with a helpless shrug.

"What are you saying, girl?" asked Alicia, looking angry.

"I'll talk to you later, Rune," Miyu sighed, laying back down in bed and pulling the blankets back around her.

"You don't believe me?" I asked, feeling helpless...and exhausted.

"Come on, baby. You can talk to Miyu later," Daxon murmured, leading me past Alicia who was glaring at me, obviously thinking I'd been making up tales.

Daxon and I walked back to the inn in silence. "I almost

had a heart attack when you weren't there this morning," he admitted almost shyly when we got to the entrance. "I thought——"

"You thought I'd left," I finished for him. I touched his face softly. "If I ever leave, I promise to say goodbye first."

"And I promise to always hunt you down and bring you back," Daxon snarled before leveling me with a kiss that sent me soaring, and for a brief moment, I wished it would last forever.

4

WILDER

Daylight settled around me, while a cold breeze kicked up leaves and dirt.

I sought fresh air, to curl my hands around grass, to sprint through the woods. I couldn't explain the heavy need as I'd been standing outside for the past hour and that call in the pit of my stomach only deepened.

But with it came a strange, unrelenting ache throughout my body where everything burned. My legs, my muscles, my chest. Including my wolf, who'd remained surprisingly quiet recently.

I put it down to the exhaustion of the fire I'd fought days ago to extinguish my home, after which I filtered through the chaos for anything that might have survived. Nothing was salvageable.

My head had been foggy soon after that day, memories growing patchy.

I lost my mind over the fire and my mother's death. After those tragedies was when I really struggled to remember everything clearly. They said loss made you forget things. Maybe that was me. Though lately, it seemed like I'd forgotten conversations and moments in my life.

It was fucking trauma, I kept telling myself. Except, I'd lost so much more in the past and it had never affected me this way. I groaned to myself, deciding I'd head into the woods and unleash my wolf. Run all day and night, anything to shake off this fucking strangling feeling like I lived inside a bubble.

I glanced down, realizing I'd been clenching my hands, knuckles gone white. I unfurled my fingers, the burning tension easing. I ground my teeth, hating this sensation, how my body and wolf weren't exactly listening to me.

I stared ahead at the town of Amarok, at some of my pack members wandering around from their homes, strolling into town. So many had their shoulders curled forward, heads low. The fear in town had escalated with the threat of a killer on the loose, and with hunters showing up. Their once-safe home was now showing signs of cracking, and I had to find a way to fix this. To ensure Amarok remained a haven for all.

After my cabin burned down, I moved into an empty place at the edge of town, until I worked out where I'd set up my new home. A few setbacks, but I would show my pack things were changing for the better soon.

The wind swished past, and something stirred inside me, causing me to lift my gaze across the river where I spotted her.

Flowing white hair billowed across her back, her blue dress fluttering around her thighs. She was a tiny thing.

My heart beat faster at the sight, with my wolf shoving forward. He pressed against my insides, demanding he come out, growled that I got closer to her. I sniffed the air, catching her scent...sweet clementines and honey. Delicious. My wolf ruffled inside me, groaning for more... longing for...

Rune.

The woman who meant nothing to me.

Who lingered on my thoughts.

Who I had planned to spend my life with. She'd made it very clear that I wasn't her forever man, and that she would rather share me. Fuck that... I'd had enough of watching her with Daxon, tired of my inner battle. When she refused to leave him for me, she'd made up both our minds. She chose him, and I accepted that. I moved on, almost forgetting her, in fact.

Watching her though, I remembered the dazed look on her face as I walked away from her, her voice breaking with heartache, her tears. I shouldn't care... I didn't care, yet I couldn't stop studying her either.

My pulse raced, every inch of me alert to her presence. I didn't pull away, though, but I was more frantic because I couldn't work out my body's reaction to her. Or why my wolf whined inside of me.

I shook my head. *Get your fucking shit together!*

I didn't love her. Doubt I ever did.

Still, every breath I took grew heavier, my eyes fixed on her body-clinging dress, her breasts bouncing with each rapid step. Her expressive face, those piercing blue eyes that always revealed her true feelings. Her fault was that she didn't know how to keep her emotions within herself; she wore them on her sleeve.

There was something captivating about studying the way she walked so gracefully, her being unaware that I observed her every move. The way she chewed on her lower lip, fiddled with her fingers across her stomach. But confusion spilled through me at what she awakened in me when I loved someone else... I loved Daria.

If I was one thing, it was being fucking loyal.

And yet with Rune... I felt things I shouldn't. I felt lost.

She confused me.

Rune fled quickly across the lawn, glancing over her shoulder where no one followed.

A protective growl rolled over my throat, pushing me. My skin buzzed with a need to transform, to call to her with my wolf. Except, he hadn't got the message through his thick skull that she wasn't ours. Not now. Not ever.

No matter how much he rustled inside me or how much the ache in my heart fluttered with the urge to make sense of the obsession washing over me.

Mine, my wolf growled in my head. *Mine. Mine.*

He was wrong. What time I had with her had been fleeting, and nothing more.

Yet, somewhere in the blurry pits of my mind, I pictured her crying. Her confusion at me leaving, and at how hard it had been for her. How much I fought to not go back to her and hold onto the last scrap of hope that she'd change her mind.

That shred of hope was nothing more than me being an utter fool.

I shook my head.

She and Daxon deserved each other. And me, I'd found real love with Daria. She was everything to me--the light of a thousand stars in the sky, the sun on my face, the smile on my mouth when I woke up next to her.

Love was finding someone you couldn't live without.

For too long, I'd been lost, but then I'd found Daria. But now...something rose within me for Rune, a desperation that I didn't recognize, yet it pushed heavily on my chest.

Looking at her blurred my thoughts, and she called to me. I stumbled forward.

Footsteps tapped the ground behind me, and arms curled around my chest, soft breasts pressed against my back, snapping me out of the haze.

I smiled.

"You deserve someone who truly loves you," Daria whispered in my ear, nuzzling the side of my neck and tightening her hold on me. "That's why you're with me. So, why are you out here staring at *her*?" Her voice darkened on the last word.

A guttural growl rolled through me from my wolf. *Down, boy*, I scolded him. Daria wasn't the enemy.

I twisted my head to meet her crystalline green eyes. Black hair framed around her spectacular face, perfectly contrasting against her silverish-colored skin. She was extravagant and all mine.

"Rune is a nobody. But you, my gorgeous queen, are everything to me."

She giggled and leaned in closer, kissing me, my addiction for her bursting forward. When we touched and kissed, the world dissolved around me and no one else could ever compare. Her perfect mouth, hypnotic body, and those eyes I lost myself in. I knew I'd follow her to the ends of the world if she asked me to. It just took me a while to realize what I'd almost missed out on all this time.

But it was better late than never that I finally came to my senses about Daria.

My wolf whined. Hesitation lingered at how bizarrely he behaved lately.

"I love you, and you belong to me," she breathed against my mouth, her hand running across my brow and into my hair, a hum buzzing down my spine. Suddenly, the sun burned brighter on my shoulders, the pine woods smelled sweeter, and I only had eyes for Daria. She made my world revolve.

"Come inside, I'm making pancakes," she purred. "I missed you."

"I won't be a moment," I responded, and her arms slid from my body, leaving me.

"Better not keep me waiting." She blew me a kiss.

I lifted my gaze once more to across the river. Rune was gone.

Maybe it was for the best we stayed out of each other's ways. I didn't feel like dealing with her neediness, or the confusion she brought me.

I blinked, staring out over the town, the woods surrounding us, convinced there had been something I intended to do by coming out here. Wracking my brain, I frowned, because all I could think about was Daria, pancakes, and her lips.

With a grin, I retreated, turned around, and strolled toward my cabin where my beauty waited for me in the doorway, smirking.

"I've been thinking." She stepped aside for me to enter the cabin, then shut the door behind us.

"Yeah, what's that?"

"I had an idea." She tucked her dark hair behind her fae ears, and I drew her into my arms. She was the most incredible woman... a queen after all... my queen.

The way she gazed into my eyes, I knew she loved me. No one looked at someone with such admiration without giving their heart away. She pushed her breasts against my chest, grinning, and she fit perfectly against me.

"Why do you look so suspicious?" I asked.

"I think Rune has become a burden on this pack. On

you. On me." She fluttered her eyes and stroked the side of my face. The sensations she elicited had me nodding. Fuck... I'd give her anything to keep her looking at me like only I existed in her world.

"Has she hurt you?" I asked.

Her lips tightened. "I've heard people say they fear the danger she brings to the town. And you know, there is one way of dealing with this." She ran her fingers across my chest in a zigzag pattern, moving lower, pausing at my belt buckle.

My breath hitched, and I admired her lips, imagining them curled around my cock.

"And what do you propose?"

"That we find a way to make your pack feel safer." She licked her lips, her hand dipping over my hardening dick. She had this way of just looking at me and my body turned to fucking fire.

"Ahm," I moan. "I'm listening."

"I think you might have no choice but to kill her."

I stiffened at her words, and a heavy sense of foreboding sloshed through me. A deep growl came from my chest, which I ignored.

"Oh, we both know once she's gone, your pack will be safe once more," Daria murmured. "She's the one bringing the hunters in here, endangering everyone." She stroked me, then leaned in to steal a small kiss. Her lips tingled against mine, and for a moment, I forgot what we were talking about.

On cue, my wolf shoved against me, snarling. And memories of Rune's sorrowful face came to mind, bringing forward those heavy feelings smothering my chest, like I'd done something horrible. But it was my wolf, constantly rejecting Daria as the woman I love, and that fucking tore me to shreds because we were meant to be one.

"What do you say?" Daria asked, pulling me out of my thoughts, cupping the side of my face with her other hand. "Imagine life back to normal in town, with you ruling. And with her gone, it might finally get rid of Daxon, as he'll most likely leave. Wouldn't that be wonderful?" Her eyes widened. "Oh, please don't say you don't like my idea? I'll be heartbroken." She pouted.

That earlier blur in my mind pulsed over me, with a cool sensation washing over me, chasing away everything else.

And my words spilled out as if of their own accord. "Of course. Anything for you."

5

RUNE

I slept for most of the day.

Somewhere deep inside, I was still coming to terms with finding ghost Rae in the town hall. I guess with the building's wretched background, it was a place that attracted spirits.

But the thing that had been on my mind was how calm he'd been, especially in comparison to his crazed attack in Daxon's basement. Rae had launched at me then, the look in his eyes filled with my death. And if he'd gotten the chance, I'd now be the dead one.

I stared out the window from my room at the Inn, at the bright moon, the stars pinned to heaven. Daxon had an errand to run, he'd said, and insisted I'd be better off here safe for a night. Which was fine, as I did feel safer here.

An abrupt knock came from the door.

I quickly turned and hurried across the room, past the empty dishes from the dinner I'd had in my room, and opened the door, half expecting it to be Daxon.

But instead, it was Miyu. With her curly, red hair pulled

back into a messy ponytail, she wore a grungy sweatshirt and jeans, her hands deep in her pocket.

"Hey, girl," she said, her lips curling into a strained smile. Her cheeks were rosy, and her eyes were rimmed red. "I figured you could help me. Hope you don't mind that I came over so late." She walked straight into my room, and I stepped aside quickly to give her space.

"Of course. What's going on?" I shut the door and turned to her, my stomach doing that thing where it clenched really hard. She'd experienced enough heartache, and I dreaded hearing something else had happened to her.

She wiped her eyes, and I moved closer, taking her into my arms and hugging her. My heart splintered even more, but she wasn't falling apart. She actually pulled away.

"I wish I could take away all your pain," I murmured, remembering the agony of my mother dying, but that was a different kind of agony to losing your soulmate. That right there was devastation that ruined lives.

I knew all about that too.

Alistair's rejection came to mind first, although that had obviously been a blessing in disguise. Followed by Wilder's more recent one, a pain that hurt far worse than being rejected by my fated mate ever had. My breaths caught in my lungs just thinking about it. I hated him for leaving me for her.

A soft hand touched my arm and snapped me out of my daze.

"You okay?" Miyu asked, concern pinched between her eyes.

I nodded. "Sometimes, it's hard to get Wilder out of my mind." But I shook my head, feeling awful talking about my own problems. "Let's forget about that. I don't want to talk about him or me. Tell me what I can help with?" I collected her hands in mine and guided her to the bed where we sat.

She gave me a wonky smile. "Sometimes I wonder if life would be simpler and less painful if there was no such thing as love."

My heart constricted. "Babe, it would be such a very sad world without love. Because then I couldn't tell you that I love you as my best friend."

She squeezed my arm and tried to smile, but it didn't stick. Blowing out a long breath, she said, "So, I've been thinking about what you said last night, and I want you to go with me to the Town Hall tonight. I-I want to speak to Rae." Her voice was barely a whisper as a tear rolled free from the corner of her eye.

"Are you sure?"

She sucked in a deep breath. "Staying in the house is making me sick, and everything reminds me of him. If I see him, talk to him, it might be easier. And I got the key just in case it's locked." Wiping the tears from her cheek with the heel of her hand, she held my gaze. Deep and glistening with tears. There was nothing I could have said to change her mind, and I worried about getting her hopes up.

But maybe a bit of time out of my room wasn't such a bad thing.

"Okay, if that will help you." I glanced over to the clock on the bedside table... past nine p.m. Not too late.

Miyu jumped to her feet, smiling and hopeful, practically bouncing on her toes. "Thank you. Thank you so much." She hugged me quickly, then rushed for the door and tore it open.

I knew it was a bad idea then, but I still stepped into my boots and grabbed a jacket, unable to say no.

Outside, I dragged on my jacket and did up the buttons

as an icy cold wind blew through my hair. "It must be snowing somewhere," I remarked.

"Probably in the mountains." Miyu walked alongside me, her hands back into her pockets, our elbows brushing together. "We get the freezing air down here. Winter's close, that means. Rae and I used to always go skiing..."

I looped my arm through hers. "Maybe we could go. I've never skied in my life. I might fall over and be an embarrassment, but I'm willing to try."

She half-smiled, and we kept on walking until she strangely took her arm away from mine. I told myself not to read too much into it. She was grieving.

We passed others who kept their heads low as they passed us, which I preferred. So many remained scared of the Hunters and blamed me.

I was getting used to it at this point.

Toward the end of the street, the town hall came into view, and I felt a sense of trepidation. I had no idea if Miyu would be able to see him, or what if he wasn't in such a good mood but reverted back to that monster he'd been before he died?

I didn't want Miyu to see him that way. She deserved so much more.

"Almost there," she said, hurrying along. I kept up with her, pushing against the wind that picked up, my nose cold. We crossed the main road, empty of cars, toward the dark brick building with a pointy roof covered in green ivy. Darkness yawned from behind the long, arched windows.

The town hall wasn't my favorite place in Amarok. Memories from there were always filled with arguments with the town packs, with finding a dead body, with ghosts now. Not to mention, Daxon telling me the figure I'd seen in the woods behind the town hall weeks ago, was not Rae.

Unease curled in my gut as we crossed the lawn. A single light remained lit above the front doors, stealing away the shadows. Behind the building, darkness lingered, along with the woods.

A shiver crawled up my spine as I remembered the figure I'd seen in the woods days ago.

I followed Miyu up the front steps as she jammed the key into the lock and pulled open the door. "Are you ready?" she asked over her shoulder, a sense of dread on her face too.

"Of course." I swallowed my worries and strolled in after her. She edged to the left, and in seconds, the lights flicked on in an empty hall with stacked chairs against the walls. Up ahead stood a stage. The place looked bare and strange with no one else there, just as it had the other night. It also smelled of mothballs and old socks mostly.

"Okay," she said, staring at me expectantly, moving slowly around the room, her head swinging left and right. "Rae, are you here?"

"I can't see him yet," I said, pushing the hair out of my face, not exactly sure how calling ghosts worked. "Maybe we keep talking to him, to see if he'll appear?"

"Rae? If you're here, please talk to me," I said out loud, then crossed the room, studying the corners and even peering outside in the yard in case he hung out there.

There was nothing unusual about the night or the town hall. No strange feelings in the air either.

Miyu's voice came from across the room, and I caught part of her whispered words. "I never thought I'd go through life without you, Rae. We were meant to be together, like the old grumpies in town, doing what we wanted, and everyone forgave us." She sniffed, and my chest squeezed. I turned away, not wanting to listen in on her message to Rae. It wasn't for my ears.

As I turned, a coldness settled over my arms. Movement snagged my focus to the back corner, away from Miyu. The two young ghosts I'd seen in the town hall weeks ago stood there. Like before, they wore white dresses and kerchief head coverings, holding each other's hands, transparent enough for me to see the rest of the hall right through their bodies. Their eyes and facial structures were almost identical, and I might have guessed they were twins if one didn't look a few years younger. But sisters they definitely had to be.

They giggled, staring at me as if I was the oddity in the room.

Maybe I should have been scared, but I was too busy being intrigued, so I walked over to them. "Hello there," I said softly.

"You're the wolf girl," the shorter girl with two plaits said in a small chipmunk voice.

"The new one, Arcadia. She keeps talking about you," her sister added.

The younger girl covered her ears, shaking her head. "She says so many bad things about you. Bad, bad, cussin'."

"I'd suggest you don't listen to her," I muttered. "Better you don't spend time with her either." Even as a ghost, Arcadia has no limitation to her craziness. She was now badgering young girls with her jealousy.

"So hard! You can't stop where she'll go, but she's angry."

"Well, until the other day when she laughed like crazy," the younger girl said.

Then they both looked at me with huge eyes. "You need to know," the older sister continued. "She burned down the cabin. Burnt it good. She wanted you to stay in there when the flames came."

I shifted my gaze from one sister to the next as their words sank in. "Arcadia burned Wilder's cabin? I knew it... she tried to kill me." My voice croaked, coming out breathy. Of course she did. I'd seen her briefly outside the kitchen window, but to know that even in death, she kept coming after me, had me covered in goosebumps. How in the world was I supposed to stop a ghost?

Fury rose through me that, no matter what I did, I couldn't get rid of her.

Because I didn't have enough people trying to kill me. Add a psychopath ghost to the mix.

"Rune," Miyu called out, her heavy footfalls hitting the floorboards as she raced up behind me. "Is that Rae?"

Coldness seeped through to my bones as she brushed up against me. I looked over to fresh tears glistening on her face.

"It's not him, but two young spirit girls I've seen here before." When I turned back to them, they were gone, and I frowned. I should have asked them about Rae. Hindsight really was a bitch.

I winced and turned to my friend, reaching over to touch her arm, but she brushed me away. "Make Rae appear. Ask the girls. You said you spoke to him," she cried, her agony slicing through me.

Woodenly, I nodded. I wouldn't argue with her. "I'll try." And I glanced back to where I'd spoken to the two ghosts. "Hello, will you speak to me again? I have a question for you. Have you seen Rae? He was here last night." I winced as no reply came.

We waited, and the longer we did, the more frantic Miyu grew. She paced and sobbed in her hands, then screamed at me some more. But I took it. I let her deal with grief how she needed to.

Until she dropped onto her ass in the middle of the room, folding her legs in front of her, lowering her head. She didn't cry; she just fell quiet.

"Miyu?" I joined her, kneeling in front of her, placing a hand on her leg. "We can keep trying every night until he returns."

She raised her head at the sound of my voice. "What if he doesn't?" There was a tremble in her words. "What if he doesn't want to see me?"

"Don't say that. Of course he does. The things he said to me last night about you were heartbreaking. They came from a man in love with you even from beyond the grave."

Her mouth thinned as she reached into the back pocket of her jeans, retrieving a small, black notebook.

"I found this in Rae's bottom drawer, under all his shirts just as you said he told you."

"Did you read it? What does it say?" I stared at the way her hand shook while holding the book, how white her knuckles turned.

She shrugged. "It's his journal, I think, but it's mostly ramblings, and I can't make sense of most of it." She cracked it open, the spine giving a small groan with how tight she gripped the notebook. Black ink writings covered both pages in a messy script. Some of the lines were horizontal, others running diagonally. She flicked through the book, and every page was exactly the same. The writing was written almost aggressively. The pages had tiny holes where he'd pushed the pen so hard, it had gone through.

I leaned in, but it was hard to read illegible handwriting upside down.

"What does it talk about? Does it have dates on his entries?" I leaned forward as she kept flipping the pages.

Then she paused on one like she'd found something.

"There are no dates, but the whole thing is filled with thoughts, so he must have been writing in it for a while. The bits I've been able to make out talk about him waking up some mornings and not knowing where he is, like he didn't recognize his own home. Other times, he'd wake up in the woods during the day and couldn't remember a thing about how he got there. He often found strange cuts and bruises on his body. There was blood on his clothes. How confused he felt, like he was going crazy."

My palms turned slick, and I wiped them down my legs. I couldn't get the feral look in his eyes out of my head. Plus, Daxon found Rae near the woods attacking a girl. Something hadn't been right with Rae for months... maybe years for all I knew. That book might hold the answers.

"Has Rae ever shown signs of losing control of his wolf or of it controlling him?" I asked.

She shook her head, staring down at the book. "He's always been the kindest person I've ever known." She looked up to meet my gaze. "But you know what's odd about this?" Her lips pursed.

"What's that?"

"In the notebook, he kept mentioning you. Never me." Her head lifted. "That's strange, right?"

Her words came at me fast, her accusation clear, and my heart raced. "W-what do you mean? What did he say about me?" Scenes of him attacking me burst through my mind. Had he had his eye on me all this time to hurt me?

I reached for the journal, needing to read his comments myself, but Miyu scrambled to her feet, taking the book out of my reach.

"This doesn't make sense," she murmured to herself, backing away from me as if worried I'd steal the notebook from her. "He kept saying he had to get close to you." Her arms dropped by her side, while her expression darkened. "What is he talking about, Rune?"

Her words seized me, bloated out my thoughts, replaced with the sheer terror of what Rae meant. Of what Miyu was asking me.

"I don't know how to answer that. I never spent a lot of time with him at the diner, so I don't understand why he'd write about me."

"Liar," she shouted, and I flinched. Anger twisted her face. "You had an affair with him, didn't you?" she spat the furious words. "How could you, Rune? I thought we were friends."

"Miyu, I would never do that to you." My throat choked and my stomach hurt badly. "You know how much I have going on with Daxon and Wilder."

She rolled her eyes. "Yeah, you stole them from Arcadia and then took both of them for yourself. If that's not greedy, I don't know what is. So, for all I know, you decided to lure in my husband as well."

My face heated up, my hands shaking. "How could you say that? That's really hurtful. I told you secrets I never revealed to anyone because I trusted you. I've never had a real friend, so you're wrong if you'd think I would go with Rae behind your back."

"Then why are you all over in his notebook? Why doesn't he mention me?" She waved the book between us now, tears drenching her cheeks.

Shit. Shit. Shit. "I know it sounds bad, but I don't know why he mentioned me. Maybe he wanted to hurt me."

"Yeah, sure! Just tell me the truth, Rune, because I've

been going insane today trying to work this out." She was almost yelling, her chin quivering.

My breaths raced, but I couldn't lose my mind. She was grieving, jumping to wild conclusions, but I had to understand why Rae would mention me at all in his journal. Why did he attack me in Daxon's basement?

"Let me study the book, please, Miyu. Between us, we can work out the truth of what was going on with Rae."

"There was nothing wrong with him," she yelled, stuffing the notebook into her back pocket. "No more lies. I deserve the truth."

There was a painful lump stuck in my throat. The truth?

What was the truth...that Daxon found him and killed him for it. That there was something so wrong with Rae when I'd seen him last, he was like a different person.

I couldn't even bring myself to tell Miyu that Daxon was the reason Rae died in the end. And I watched it happen. If she hated me now, she'd want me dead too if she found out the truth.

Guilt wrecked me. It tore me to shreds to see her falling apart, and I did withhold the truth from her. But it wasn't what she expected. And I wouldn't tell her... not in her state. Even if her earlier words and accusations hurt...

I squared my shoulders, meeting her gaze despite being unable to stop crying. "I never had an affair with Rae. Nothing happened between us. I swear on my life. But I think something was wrong with Rae. Why else would he write a journal like that?"

Her glare at me intensified. All the softness in her eyes faded, and instead, I stared at someone who hated me. Who blamed me. Who was drowning in grief.

"Miyu..."

She recoiled from my outstretched arm. "Some of the

most dangerous people around you are those who lie and think they are telling the truth." She whipped around and rushed out of the town hall.

I burst into tears, my insides feeling like they were broken, like glass shattering. I took a step forward, hating Miyu's accusations and terrified of why Rae scribbled in his journal about me.

I couldn't even ask him about it anymore. Rushing forward, I hugged myself and plunged into the cold night, running back to the inn.

6

DAXON

I'd always been the type of wolf to obsess over sparkly things. Rune had started out like that, another obsession.

And then she'd become my only obsession.

And now she was slipping away.

It was obviously inconvenient for her to find out about my little killing hobby, and for it to be her best friend's mate that I was killing. But we would get through this. We had to get through this.

There wasn't any other option for me.

So here I was, walking towards the inn to convince the girl that was destined to be my mate to go on a fucking picnic with me since I could barely get her to speak to me at the moment.

I was obviously desperate.

Across the street, I spotted an unfamiliar man chatting with Ms. Flenderson and the rest of her knitting group. They were all ancient, and they all had eyes for him. I slipped into the shadows of the alleyway so that I could watch him closer without being obvious.

The guy was about my height, wearing a black leather jacket that Wilder would have been jealous of.

The douchebag.

His gaze flicked over to where I was, and his smirk widened, like he knew what I was doing. I bared my teeth, trying to control the urge I had to stalk him and tie him up in my basement. I was taking a break from that for the moment.

At least until I could convince Rune to love me again.

But I could kill him in the woods if I needed to, rip him apart with my wolf. Rune seemed to be alright with that type of killing.

I sniffed the air, trying to get a read on him. He wasn't her asshole's goons, I could tell that just from here. He was too...shiny, too polished. He was also too out in the open. The goons and the hunters who had come so far had stayed in the shadows. This guy was too brazen, parading out in the middle of the day, in the middle of Main Street.

His gaze flicked again to where I was standing, and I strode back out to the sidewalk, making sure I gave him a challenging stare as I did so. His grin only broadened as he said something that made Ms. Flenderson fucking giggle. Ms. Flenderson never giggled.

I pulled out my phone and debated. I wasn't going to cancel my date with Rune, but the stranger also needed to be checked out.

A text to asshole it was.

There's a new guy in town. I need you to check him out, I wrote to Wilder even though what I really wanted to do was reach through my phone and choke the guy.

Wilder: Fine.

I growled at Wilder's flippant answer before putting my phone in my pocket. I threw one last warning glare at the guy, and then satisfied that our retirement population wasn't suddenly going to be massacred, I set off towards the inn once again.

I should have been over the moon that Wilder was out of the picture. This had been what I had wanted all along. But it just so happened that the only person I cared about on the whole planet was Rune.

And she was devastated. Her sadness was so palpable I could taste it in the air. I breathed it in every time I was with her. It permeated every inch of her. She was listless… depressed. I could keep on hoping that she'd move on from Wilder, forget him like somehow he'd managed to forget her based on the town rumors I'd been hearing everywhere, but I didn't think it would happen.

Just like I didn't think it was possible for Rune to walk away from me, even with what she'd seen.

We were under her skin, embedded in her heart like a knife. If Wilder didn't get his head out of his ass, he was going to ruin everything.

I knew there was more to everything going on. Wilder wasn't a cheater, as annoying as it was to admit. But that was a situation I'd have to look more into later. First, I had to fix Rune and me.

Starting right now.

I made my way into the Inn, nodding at Carrie who was polishing the wooden bar. Her eyes flashed in fear for a second before she gave me a hesitant smile and busied herself with her task.

I strode up the stairs, clenching tightly to the flowers that I'd brought in hopes they could make her smile.

I could do this wooing thing. I was great at it. I could charm her until she forgot all the bad parts about me.

The only problem is, I wanted her to love all my bad parts. I'd thought that she could.

I knocked on the door, feeling a bit nervous. She opened it a second later, smiling at me shyly as she stood in the doorway.

Fuck, she was beautiful.

I had to adjust the front of my pants like a randy sixteen-year-old boy just from one look at her. She was wearing tight black leggings with a light blue top that perfectly showcased her fucking perfect tits. Her top was low cut, and my wolf and I were in total agreement that this date needed to end with a sleepover...or a fuck in the woods.

I would literally take anything at this point.

"Hi," she said hoarsely, and my lust dimmed a bit when I realized that her hoarseness was because she'd been fucking crying again.

"Baby," I said, before grabbing her and pulling her into my arms. I buried my face in her hair, trying to calm myself down by taking in big gulps of her scent. It was still muted from the fae bitch's voodoo spell, but she still smelled fucking amazing.

I was squeezing her too hard, but it felt like she was a step away from disappearing forever. I was not the kind of wolf that abided by the whole "if you love someone, let them go." Fuck that. If she ever did leave, I would hunt her down to the ends of the earth.

I sounded a bit like her psycho ex right now, but while he wanted to keep her and pin her wings like a caged butterfly, I wanted to help her fly. I just wanted to fly with her.

I hadn't been sleeping well lately. Every time I fell asleep I would wake up in a panic that something had happened to her. She'd tried to send me back to my place the last few nights, and inevitably, I'd ended up skulking around the inn, unsettled unless I knew she was nearby.

Right at that moment, with her in my arms was the only time that I could feel a semblance of peace.

"Ready to go?" I asked gently, taking one last inhale for good measure before reluctantly separating from her.

"Yeah," she said softly, with a smile that didn't quite reach her eyes.

I decided that this date wasn't going to end until her smile was real.

I may be a psychopath, completely uncaring if the world burned, but I would do anything to make her happy.

Anything.

"Where are we going?" she asked as we set off down the street towards my car. There was a waterfall a few miles away that had magical properties that I'd discovered as a boy. It was where I went to decompress and be alone...well, there and my basement, obviously.

"It's a surprise," I told her with a wink, and I grinned in satisfaction when her lips flushed and I could smell the faint scent of her arousal.

At least I could confirm she was still attracted to me after everything.

I helped her into my car and we drove down the street. She spent most of the time staring out the window, her head leaning against the seat and her shoulders slumped.

I spent most of the time watching her and trying not to run us off the road as I did so.

I turned off the road and parked before opening her door. "I guess I should have asked if you were good for a short little hike," I told her sheepishly. I'd been so focused on how fucking amazing she looked that I'd forgotten to check she had on proper shoes. I glanced down quickly and saw it was my lucky day--she was wearing a pair of black sneakers.

I really needed to get my head in the game.

"I'm always up for a hike," she said, a trace of excitement in her voice. I grabbed her hand and squeezed it before sneaking in one more kiss as we began to walk. The path that led to the waterfall didn't start for half a mile. On the day I'd even discovered the place, I'd been out for a run while shifted, and it had been just luck that I stumbled upon it.

We didn't talk much as we walked. The weather was crisp and cool, and it was the best time of the year to be outside.

I pointed out a fairy ring that used to be a portal to their world, but of course, that just makes her sad because it reminds her of Wilder and Daria.

We finally made it to the waterfall, the white, frothy cascades of water an enchanting sight, but not one that beat watching Rune's eyes widen in delight as she took it all in. A little squeal escaped her perfect mouth.

"This place is incredible," she exclaimed, throwing her arms around me. I set down the backpack I'd been carrying on the ground as she ran to the water's edge. There were three waterfalls that all poured into the lake in front of us. The water was a vivid shade of turquoise that changed in intensity through the summer as the snow caps melted. I'd never seen anything like it. This place was a true natural wonderland. The rocky outcroppings, the lichen, the moss, the lush grass that surrounded the pool, the way the spray of the waterfall created miniature rainbows everywhere...

Pretty good place for a date.

She pulled off her shoes and dipped her toes into the

water tentatively, expecting it to be cold as it should have been at this time of year.

"Holy hell, it's warm," she called out, looking back at me in amazement.

That was just another mystery of this place. The water was always warm, just a few degrees cooler than a hot tub year-round.

"We're swimming, right?" she asked.

"Only if we do it without clothes," I quipped back, and she smirked with me.

Yep, I was getting lucky.

After standing in the shallow water for a few minutes, looking around at everything, she got out and walked over to where I'd spread out a blanket and some food.

"You planned a picnic?" she asked in a soft, breathy voice that never ceased to make me hard. There was an edge of vulnerability laced through her words, like she couldn't believe anyone would ever make an effort to do anything special for her.

"Of course, baby. I wanted to make you smile today. I'd do anything for you, even cook."

She melted against me and her whole body relaxed as I gently rubbed her back. A second later, her stomach rumbled and she pulled away from me, a faint blush to her cheeks.

"Perfect timing for lunch," I said with a wink, even as I noted how thin she looked. How had she lost that much weight in the last few days? I needed to start making sure she was eating.

I pulled out the small cooler I'd stuffed in my backpack and started to unload the turkey croissant sandwiches, chips, carrots, and strawberries that I'd packed for our date. I handed Rune a sandwich, and she immediately took a big bite, much to my wolf's satisfaction. He liked seeing his soon-to-be mate fed.

My stomach clenched thinking about making Rune my mate. She kept rejecting my bite, and that was when things were relatively good between us. What were the chances that she would accept my bite with everything happening right now?

It didn't seem likely. My wolf snarled at the thought, and I silently agreed with him. That wasn't an option.

"This is really good!" she told me as she inhaled the rest of the sandwich. I immediately gave her another, desperate to get as much food inside her as possible. She smirked like she knew what I was doing but began eating the sandwich anyway. The rest of lunch went well. She pretended not to notice how I kept loading up her plate, and I pretended that I wasn't watching every move she made.

We were both winners.

When she finished eating, she shifted uncomfortably, like she had bad news to tell me, and dread crept up my spine.

"What is it?" I asked gently as she fiddled with the blanket.

"It's probably nothing. But Miyu found Rae's journal… and there was some really weird stuff inside of it," she began.

"What kind of stuff?" I asked, frowning at the mention of Rae.

A tear slipped down her cheek. "Stuff about me. Miyu thinks that Rae and I were having an affair. She hates me."

My wolf wanted to burn the whole world just thinking about Rune with Rae, even though I knew with everything inside of me that it would never have happened.

"She's just going through grief. There's a bunch of

stages that come with that. Miyu seems to have skipped to anger."

Rune shrugged her shoulders, like she wasn't sure I was right but was hoping that I was. "What he wrote about me, it had to have been bad for her to jump to that kind of conclusion. I mean, I thought Miyu knew me. And Rae would never have done that. He only had eyes for her."

I cracked my neck uncomfortably, trying to decide exactly what to say. "You know that you created quite a stir coming to town. There were...a lot of interested shifters."

She frowned and laughed before she realized that I was being serious. "No one ever talked to me, let alone flirted with me."

I raised my eyebrow. "You were dating the two alphas of the town, two alphas that don't like to share based on past experience. I don't think they were going to try something with the two of us around."

She frowned, the news obviously upsetting her. "But Rae would never have..." she began.

I nodded my head, wanting to agree with her and make her feel better. But the truth was, I had no idea who Rae was. I certainly never would have thought him capable of everything he'd done. I'd never really paid attention to him before, not until Rune wanted to start doing double dates with him. And he had always seemed devoted to Miyu in those moments. I needed to get a hold of that journal though.

"It's alright, baby. I'm sure it will all blow over. She's just not thinking clearly right now. She knows who you are," I said soothingly, taking her hand in mine and softly rubbing her skin.

She nodded glumly, a few more tears falling. I reached into the cooler and brought out the slices of vanilla cake that I knew she was obsessed with. I watched in gratification as her eyes lit up, showing that I was successfully distracting her, and for the next few minutes we didn't say anything as we took turns feeding each other bites of cake.

———

After we were done with the cake, she laid down on the blanket and closed her eyes, stretching her arms above her and basking in the perfect, cloudless day.

"I'm pretty sure this is what I want my heaven to look like," she moaned, the sound not intended to be sexual but still making me hard nevertheless. She stayed like that for a long moment, looking completely at peace for the first time in what felt like forever.

Her eyes suddenly popped open and her gaze went to me. "How about a swim?" she asked, slowly getting up and standing in front of me. I watched, tongue-tied, as she slipped off her shirt, then her leggings, until she was standing in front of me in a pale pink bra that was completely see-through, showcasing her dusky nipples that I was suddenly salivating over...and a matching pale pink thong.

I groaned and wiped my hand down my face. "Sweetheart, you're literally killing me right now."

She didn't answer me, just hit me in the face with her thong and then her bra, and I watched as she walked slowly towards the water's edge, taking a few steps into the water before looking back at me. "Are you coming?" she asked.

"I hope so," I quipped, nearly tearing off my clothes in an effort to get there as fast as possible.

I strode after her, not even bothering to hide how eager

I was to be with her. If she'd let me, I'd never leave her side. That's how gone I was over this girl.

She dunked herself under the water before breaking the surface and somehow managing that perfect hair flip I'd thought could only be done in the movies.

"I can't get over how warm this water is," she beamed. She looked like some kind of water nymph with her pale hair and breathtaking blue eyes that almost matched the color of the water.

I was pretty much done waiting at that point.

"Ready to get wet?" I asked, reaching out and pulling her body through the water towards mine until she was plastered against me.

"I thought I already was," she said with a smirk.

"Not nearly wet enough," I purred. She shivered against me, and I rolled my hips, making sure she could feel every inch of my hard cock.

She moaned against me, and I began to slide my hands all over her smooth skin, watching as she got that dazed, needy look that I loved. I slid some of my fingers between her legs, gliding softly along her folds before gently massaging her clit.

"This still mine?" I growled.

"Yes," she whimpered breathlessly, her lips parting as a flush spread up her neck that had nothing to do with the temperature of the water.

Her thighs wrapped around my waist, ankles locking behind my back as she opened herself to me further. Her arms slid across my chest, and I just wanted her touching me all over.

I wanted her to make as many of those sexy, whimpered, helpless noises as I could get out of her.

Rune bit her lip as I moved my hands out from between

her legs. I watched as her face softened again. This was the only time that she actually opened up to me, where she lowered her defenses. Before the unfortunate situation with Rae, I had wondered if it was the demons from her asshole ex that was holding her back, and now I wondered if it was just me in general.

But all that didn't matter right now, while she was arching back, showcasing her pretty throat to me like I wasn't an alpha that could strike at any moment.

A growl of satisfaction burst out of my chest as my fingers dug into her hips and yanked them forward, plunging into her tight, perfect pussy. Forget just being by her side every minute of every day, I wanted to be like this every minute.

"Daxon," she cried out as I pulled out slowly and watched the way her pussy gripped at me.

I thrust inside of her, and she trembled and clenched around me so tightly that I was afraid I was going to come already.

"That's my pretty girl. You feel so perfect around my cock."

She whimpered at my dirty words, and even in the water, I could feel how sopping wet she was.

Perfection.

She clenched again, and I held my breath as I tried to get control of myself. Did she know that she owned me? Did she know that she had the power to bring me to my knees at any second?

Her blue eyes watched me, roving over my face until they landed on my lips. I'd known she'd loved me for a while now. Even when she hadn't admitted it, I'd known it. But right now...right now she looked like she was desperate for me, and I couldn't help but slam into her harder, her desire pushing me into a frenzy.

Everything I felt for her was rushing through me at once —love, possession, and desperate primal fucking need. My insides felt like pure madness. I never wanted it to end.

My pace was slowed by the water as I pulled out, then thrust back in, making sure I went in all the way to the hilt. She was a goddess with her eyes half-lidded, lips parted, making those sexy little moans I always found myself craving like an addict craving a hit of cocaine.

"Daxon," she breathed. Her hands gripped the back of my neck, pulling, directing me down to her chest, and of course...I obeyed immediately.

I caught her nipple in my mouth, suckling and drawing on her sensitive flesh, greedy, possessive gratification flowing through me. I loved the way she responded to me. I worked her nipples roughly with lips, tongue, and teeth until she was writhing against me, mindless with lust.

"I love you so fucking much," I rasped against her skin, my wolf desperate for us to move a little farther up and try a mating mark once again. "You're mine. You'll always be mine. Tell me you'll never leave me."

A soft whining sound escaped her throat as she trembled in my arms and fell over the edge, somehow tightening even more on my aching cock as her orgasm spiraled through her.

"Say it," I ordered as I sucked harder on her tender nipple, eliciting another soft cry that was music to my ears.

"Yes," she practically sobbed as I continued to move in and out of her. "I love you."

"And you'll stay with me. Always," I directed, extending my fangs so that I could run them gently across her skin, making her whimper even more.

"I'll stay. Always," she moaned. Her hands fisted in my hair, pulling as I moved one of my hands down in between us to circle her clit and send her into another orgasm.

The water was splashing around us in small tidal waves as we continued to move. Her soft moans and desperate breaths drowned out the sound of the waterfall crashing nearby. All I could hear was her. All I could see was her.

Her muscles trembled and she began to chant breathlessly. "Please, please, please. Daxon. Please." I loved her fucking voice. Loved everything about her. I pulled her even closer to me with one arm around her waist before fisting her hair and bringing her lips to me in a hungry, almost violent kiss. Our tongues battled against each other. Was she feeling it? Did she understand this connection between us? That I would do anything to make her happy, to keep her satisfied, to keep her mine.

"I love you," I breathed into her mouth again.

Her breath caught in her throat as I somehow pressed in deeper until I'd pushed all the way to the base, her clit pressing against my lower abs, thrusting deep in a pulsing rhythm. Her eyes closed as her mouth fell open in a soundless moan against my lips, and I knew I couldn't hold on much longer. Her nails dug into my back as I slowed our ravenous kiss, savoring every slow lick. The taste of her was nirvana, better than anything I'd ever experienced.

"Daxon," she cried out as her body quaked against mine, once again clamping down on me as another orgasm hit her. This time, I couldn't stop myself; I pushed deep as my muscles tensed, and I came long and hard inside of her.

Our breaths tangled together as our foreheads touched, and we slowly came down from the high that we'd just experienced.

"Wow," she finally said in a gasp, her pupils still blown

out from all the orgasms I'd just given her. My wolf was very pleased about that.

She stared at my face again, searching for something. I didn't know what she was looking for, but I'd have given her anything she asked. Anything but her freedom from me that is.

I reluctantly pulled out of her, and we both groaned at the sensation. I immediately missed the feel of her and contemplated a way to spend the rest of the day inside her.

I pushed some hair out of her face that had fallen, and I watched in awe at the happiness I could see in her expression.

But just with that thought, the light slowly started to fade, and I knew that Wilder had just crept back into her thoughts.

"Should we do some cliff jumping?" I asked, desperate to distract her some more.

She eyed the rocks by the waterfall doubtfully before nodding her head. "Let's do it."

We spent the next hour climbing the rocks and jumping into the perfect water. We jumped until her laughter was ringing through the air continuously and I was convinced I'd never had a better day.

We were wading in the pool of water right in front of the waterfall, her legs wrapped against me as I tried to convince myself I couldn't slide into her yet with how hard I'd gone before. Her hair was spread out in the water behind her like some perfect fucking mermaid, and little prisms of the rainbows from the waterfall were reflected on her features.

"I don't want this day ever to end," she said with a sigh, eyeing the fact that the sun was starting to sink lower in the sky and we still had to hike back to the car. She squeezed me tighter. "Let's shift and go for a run," she exclaimed. "Just a small one."

I was already swimming us both over to the shore, thinking a shift sounded perfect. We were already naked, so we were ready to go.

She tensed up and began her shift but stopped as a stream of blood began to pour out of her nose. She wiped at the blood, confused, a flicker of fear falling across her face.

"This happened last time I shifted too," she murmured as blood continued to fall.

I tried to put on a brave face, but I was a bit concerned too. There was so much that we still didn't know about Rune, and it felt like we were no closer than before to figuring it all out. Was this a byproduct of what Daria had done, or was it related to the super heat she'd been in...or was it something else?

"Maybe it's just because you haven't been taking care of yourself," I suggested lamely. "I'm going to be watching you even closer now to make sure you're eating and sleeping. Well, even closer than I already have been," I added, knowing that my stalker mode had definitely been engaged as of late.

A ghost of a smile crossed her lips as she wiped up the last trickle of blood that had fallen. "Ready to shift?" she asked, a determined glint in her eye.

I nodded, my mind obsessing over all the things that could be wrong, but I pasted on a smile for her nevertheless. Maybe she was meant to have Wilder in her life too just because of all the trouble she attracted. It was more than a full-time job, and I was glad to do it, but sometimes I feared whatever I could do wasn't enough.

I watched as she transformed into her majestic wolf form, her movements looking a bit stiffer than normal. The sight still took my breath away, just like every time. Her fur resembled the aurora borealis as the colors from the water-fall reflected off of it. Combine that with the silver dusted pawprints she left behind her, something I'd never seen on another shifter, and it was a feast for the eyes.

She whined when she finished and paused before care-fully shaking out her fur. Had it hurt? That wasn't normal.

I quickly shifted and brushed against her, trying to comfort her, but she seemed alright as she set off on a run around the area.

Everything would be alright. I'd make sure of it.

But fuck, Wilder really needed to get his head out of his ass...soon.

———

Wilder

I was here again. Like I had been the last two nights. Outside the inn where Rune was sleeping. Daria had busi-ness to attend to in her realm, and like the terrible guy that I am, here I was stalking my ex-girlfriend.

I was hidden in the shadows, watching as she leaned on her windowsill staring at the moon, a pensive look on her beautiful face. What was she thinking about? Did she ever think about me?

And why did my wolf care so much?

My memories felt like a blur. When I thought about my time with Rune, there was nothing but confusion, bits and pieces missing until all I had were the bad times. The times where I'd felt jealous and unloved, like I could never be enough for her, like I would be forced to love her with my whole heart when I would never get anything but half of hers.

Sometimes there would be flickers of memories that felt like strangers in my head. A time where she would be laughing, where we were in bed and I was moving inside of her, her hands clutching at the sheets. I would try to grasp onto the image, and I'd immediately get a migraine so bad I'd throw up. I could remember that I'd thought that I loved her, but I couldn't remember how it felt, or when I'd felt it.

Even now, watching her, I could feel a headache forming, like my head was trying to force memories out of me that I'd somehow lost. She moved away from the window, and I leaned back against the wall I'd been standing by, wondering if I was going crazy. Maybe I had a brain tumor. Did shifters get tumors like that? My wolf was full out whining inside of me, desperate for me to barge through the doors

What did he know that I didn't know? I was in love with Daria. She was perfect for me, right? Then why did it feel like there was a schism inside of me, like a huge chunk of my soul was missing? Why was my wolf unsettled and unhappy every time I was near Daria? Why did he want to tear her into shreds every time he heard her voice?

My hands trembled as I rubbed at my face, just wanting a moment of fucking peace where I didn't feel so unsettled. This was just new relationship problems, right? From what I'd seen, Rune and Daxon were happy together. She didn't miss me at all.

That thought inevitably spiraled into others, like how I wasn't sure where Daria and I had begun and Rune and I had ended. For the first time in my life, I couldn't trust my thoughts. And it was a terrifying thing.

Hating myself, I crept out of the shadows and headed back down the street aimlessly, not having any idea of where to go and trying to ignore my wolf who was begging me to go back.

I was halfway down Main Street when I happened to look over into one of the pub windows and saw a guy I hadn't seen before.

His head was thrown back, and he was laughing while what seemed like a quarter of the town sat gathered around him, staring at him in awe like he was some kind of god.

Which in itself was strange, since this town was nothing but cautious about strangers. Look at how they'd treated Rune when she'd arrived.

My wolf growled in displeasure.

This must be the guy Daxon had texted me about. I walked closer to the pub and decided just to go in. This was my town, and I had no reason to be skulking about.

I strode in, and unlike normal, where the pub would quiet and heads would tip towards me in a gesture of respect, no one in there seemed to be aware of my existence. They were all staring at him.

I walked over to the bar, trying not to look like I was here to watch him, and gave a head nod to Dietra. She immediately walked over with a whiskey, not seeming to be as interested in Mr. Popular as everyone else in the place was.

I took a big sip and then set my glass down, savoring the burn. "This his first time in here?" I asked lowly.

Her gaze flicked to the guy briefly before coming back to me. "Apparently he's been making his way through the bars in town, gathering groupies as he goes."

"What's his name?"

She shot me a concerned look. "Aren't you and Daxon supposed to know all about new people before they start mingling with the packs?"

I huffed before taking another gulp of my drink. "It's been a busy week," I muttered, and she sighed before picking up a rag to clean up a spill a few seats down. Just then, another round of nauseous laughter filled the pub.

"His name is Ares, and he's quite something," she muttered sarcastically.

Before I could ask her what that meant, there was more laughter. Listening closely, it didn't sound like his story about his neighbor's cat being obsessed with him was all that interesting, but everyone in here seemed to disagree. His delivery was smooth, I'd give him that, and sneaking a glance at him out of the corner of my eye, I could tell that he was extremely charismatic. The girls sitting in a group to the left of him all looked like they would lift up their skirts right there at a word from him.

I was immediately suspicious.

The door swung open and Daxon sauntered in, not hiding his disdain of Ares as he shot him a glare as he walked by. Ares, in turn, just smirked at Daxon, like he knew something Daxon didn't.

Daxon slid onto the barstool next to me, and Dietra was immediately there, handing him a beer. "I hate that guy," he grumbled as he took a long swig from his bottle.

"What's he done to you?" I asked, lifting an eyebrow.

Daxon shot the stranger another look of disdain. "Nothing yet, but I've got a bad feeling about him. It's like he's cast a spell over the whole town in a day. I'm just hoping he doesn't run into Rune." I shifted uncomfortably in my seat, my wolf on edge just at the mention of her name.

Daxon gave me the same look he'd just leveled at Ares. "Not that you would care about that, right?"

I pursed my lips and took another drink.

"When are you going to man up and go talk to her?" he asked.

I glanced at him. "What?"

"You think I haven't seen you outside the inn the last few nights, watching the window to her room like it held all the secrets to life?"

I scoffed even as my wolf snickered at me.

"I don't know what you're talking about," I replied gruffly, my ears growing hot with embarrassment.

I watched as his claws extended around his beer before he retracted them.

Interesting.

We both ignored another round of laughter as Daxon shot daggers at me. "What's your problem, Daxy-boy," I said tauntingly. "Don't you have exactly what you want now?"

He leaned closer. "The only reason I'm not tearing your head off is because Rune loves it so much. I don't know what is going on with you, but this little hissy fit you've got going on...It needs to stop. For whatever reason, Rune is desperate for you. And even though you don't deserve it, I'll do whatever it takes to make her happy. Even try to fix you."

My wolf was going crazy inside of me at the notion that Rune was unhappy. My skin felt hot and itchy, and something was on the edge of my brain, but as hard as I tried, I couldn't get to it.

"How can you even stand to touch that bitch?" Daxon continued, unaware that I was falling apart at the moment. "I can't even look at another girl. They hold absolutely no interest to me. There might as well not be anyone else in existence on earth except for Rune...I thought it was that way for you too," he finished quietly.

I gripped my glass of whiskey so hard that it shattered in my hand. I stared down at the mess. The glass had made a jagged cut in my hand, and the blood was quickly beginning to pool onto the bar.

"Might want to get a bandaid on that," came a voice from next to me. I looked over and inwardly rolled my eyes at the fact that the new guy was standing next to me, staring interestedly at the blood.

"Thanks for the helpful tip," I responded dryly.

Like the helpful woman that she was, Dietra was there a second later with a clean rag.

"Good thing we heal fast," he continued. I stiffened for just a second, both relieved that he was part of the supernatural community and I didn't have to worry about keeping things from him that happened around town, and more suspicious, because whatever he smelled like wasn't familiar to me. I could smell the magic on his skin that marked him as a supernatural, but he wasn't a wolf. Or at least he wasn't completely a wolf. He didn't smell like any of the hunters had either, though.

"Yes, good thing," I finally muttered, distractedly. My cut did in fact immediately heal, and once it did, I gave Ares my attention.

"So, where you from, friend?" Daxon purred dangerously. Evidently, Daxon had brought his psycho out to play. That didn't bode well for this guy.

"Here and there. I was in the army for the last five years, and now that I'm out, I guess I'm just traveling around... seeing where I fit," Ares replied easily.

"So you'll be moving on tomorrow then, I assume?" asked Daxon, obviously trying to make it clear that Ares did not fit well here.

Ares laughed smoothly. "Everyone's been so welcoming

here. You can't help but feel at home." I could tell that Ares was intentionally trying to bait Daxon and me. I just didn't know why he was doing that.

"Well, I think I'll be calling it a night," I said casually, sliding off my bar stool and giving a nod to Dietra that I was done. She knew just to put my drink on my tab. It was kind of sad how long I'd been coming here.

"The night's young," Ares joked. "I'm still waiting for the pretty blond I ran into the other day to show her face around here. I've never seen anything like her."

My wolf snapped because we knew he was talking about Rune. Somehow, he'd met her already. I had Ares against the wall, a knife against his throat. The bar had gone dead quiet behind me.

"Woah there, buddy, I don't put out until the second date," Ares joked.

My wolf itched to slice the guy's throat and just end it there. But of course, I couldn't do that.

At least not with the eyes of everyone in town watching me.

Daxon sidled up next to me and put his arm on the wall next to Ares. "Just to be perfectly clear, the so-called blonde you mentioned...pretend like she doesn't exist. Don't talk to her, don't touch her...don't even breathe the same air as her. Are we clear?" Daxon hissed, letting out a tiny glimpse of his crazy that would have had most shifters shitting their pants.

Ares was relaxed against the wall though, with no smell of fear coating the air. He seemed awfully at ease considering two alphas were at this throat.

Another strike in the suspicious column.

Ares put up his hands. "Hey, she's taken. I didn't know,

gentlemen. But might I add, you two are awfully lucky to get that one in your bed."

My hand moved then and I "accidentally" nicked his throat. Something flashed in his eyes before he quickly shuttered the emotion.

"Sorry about that," I drawled, taking a step away and wiping the knife on Ares' shirt.

"No worries," he said in that same charming voice he'd held the whole evening. "Accidents happen."

"Yep," I quipped before nodding at everyone who was staring at us. "See you around, buddy," I said before striding slowly out of the bar followed by Daxon.

Daxon and I walked down the street a bit before he finally spoke. "Our betas need to keep an eye on that one 24/7," he hissed. I nodded and immediately took out my phone to text Marcus and the others.

Daxon headed away from me...in the direction of the inn. My wolf moaned desperately that we should follow him.

Just then Daria texted me. *See you soon.*

The words should have filled me with happiness. But all I felt was dread.

"Get your head out of your ass before it's too late," Daxon called over his shoulder.

I didn't answer him as I began to walk in the opposite direction. But I knew that I would find myself outside the inn at some point tonight. Just staring at her window. Hoping for a glimpse of the girl that I was supposed to hate.

7
RUNE

I was definitely broken.

I didn't feel right. My last transformation in the woods with Daxon hurt... and it shouldn't sting like someone was shoving blades into my side. Afterward, when I turned back, my nose had bled. Then when I attempted to shift again into my wolf form this morning, that sharpening pain returned and made transforming close to impossible. Then the nosebleed happened again. Something was wrong with me.

What if Alistair's spell was coming back over my wolf? What if he'd broken something inside me?

I wasn't a fool, and I wanted to shift without blood loss, so I hurried down the sidewalk toward the doctors', needing an answer.

My nose wrinkled at the pungent stench of garbage from an alleyway I passed, while ahead of me, the main street buzzed with people.

Locals strolled in the morning sunlight, chatting, some even laughing, while others were popping into the stores with friends, with family. It almost seemed like a normal day, despite Rae's death.

Maybe the packs in town had seen so much death that they'd become numb to it. I understood that with the constant chaos that flooded my life, but it never got easier.

With it, Miyu came to mind...my best friend, except I didn't know what we'd become now. Enemies? Strangers? Would she ever speak to me again?

Her accusations in the town hall refused to leave my thoughts, and it still burned me up that she'd thought so little of me. I would never chase after her husband. But anger had a way of making people say ugly, hurtful things.

I kept telling myself that... not that it helped. So I kept walking, needing to stop thinking about it before I drove myself nuts.

From behind a parked car, Wilder emerged without warning. His head raised and our gazes clashed at the same time, both of us paused on the sidewalk as though an invisible barrier kept us apart. By the frozen look on his face, I'd say he was just as startled as me.

My heart leapt into my throat, and I told my feet to move and get away from him, but they remained glued to the cement. Heaviness pressed in on my chest, nothing good could come of us crossing paths.

Silence filled the void, yet his powerful presence disturbed the air.

He ran a hand through his hair, his bicep muscles bulging. He kept watching me like he wanted to say something. Like he couldn't find his words. His lips thinned, and a confused expression washed over his face. For a sliver of a second, I felt stupid pity for how lost he seemed. My hands tingled with the auto-response of going to him to see if he was alright, while anguish seeped through to my soul and burned a hole right through it, leaving me breathless.

And with it, reality crashed back into me. After everything we'd been through, and what he did to me, he didn't deserve anything from me. The full extent of the grief he caused came back with a vengeance, leaving me in fragmented agony where tears already pricked my eyes.

The longer I stared at him, the more my veins turned to fire. His presence was a reminder of how shredded he left my heart. How easily he walked away from what we had and jumped into the fae queen's arms.

I hated him and Daria with every fiber of my being.

"You're in my way," I snapped at him, finding the strength to take a step forward, then another, and I had brushed right past him when he grabbed my wrist.

"Rune," he murmured, his features going blank. His mouth was partly open, but there was a war going on behind his gaze. What in the world was wrong with him?

But any confusion I held earlier was stripped from my body, and I yanked my hand from his grip. "No," I answered. "There's nothing you can say to me. You lost the privilege to talk to me, to touch me, to even look at me." My voice climbed, and my arms shook by my side.

Why did I let him affect me so much?

His brows drew together, eyes narrowing their stare on me. "Rune!"

"Is there an echo here?" I snapped.

A wild haggard look flared over his face. Gone was the uncertainty, and in its place, shadows danced under his eyes. His features seemed to morph before my eyes, which in itself was a strange change to witness firsthand, as though something had come over him.

"You've always been so needy, so weak, Rune," he spat. "If there's anything I regret, it's not leaving you earlier."

I trembled all over, goosebumps tightening my skin, and I drew in ragged breaths. "You want to talk about weakness, go look in the mirror, asshole," I countered, exhausted by his psychotic emotional swings. Daxon was the crazy one, and right now, Wilder was giving him a great run for that title.

I tore my gaze from him, turning away, but I ended up bumping right into someone else.

A man in his twenties grabbed my arm to catch my stumble. "Careful," he said with a kind smile, leaning in closer.

A sudden blur nudged right past me, shoving me aside. I stumbled, while Wilder growled like a beast, snatching the man's throat and driving him up against the wall, pinning him, strangling him.

My gut twisted with shock. I flew after them, my mind screaming that he'd kill this guy who did nothing wrong other than help me.

The man blanched, gasping for air as Wilder bellowed in his face. "Don't ever touch her again!"

"Let him go," I yelled and slammed into Wilder's side, shoving my fists into his ribs. "What the fuck is wrong with you?"

But Wilder didn't respond, didn't even look at me. Panic gripped me. I frantically stumbled back and scanned the sidewalk for something, anything to wrench him off the man.

There was nothing to use as a weapon, and with the guy's gurgled sounds, dread swallowed me. He was killing him, and there were already enough deaths in this dumb town. For not the first time, I was really questioning my decision to stay in Amarok.

Other locals were coming toward us to watch the commotion.

"Wilder, stop!" I bolted to him and did the only thing I could do to take down a mountain of a man. I kicked my foot into the back of his knee. He crumpled to the side, and I took the moment to kick his other leg.

He groaned and stumbled back, releasing the man who fell back onto his feet and started coughing for air.

I rushed to his side and seized his arm, then pulled him away. "Get out of here," I warned, and he did just that. A harrowed look was the last thing I saw as he scrambled down the sidewalk, rubbing his throat.

Wilder spun toward me, his eyes on fire, fists curled by his side.

"What the fuck!" I yelled. "You don't get to be an asshole to me, then go all protective shit on anyone who talks to me. You pushed me away, remember that!"

"Oh, Wilder," a sickly sweet voice came from behind me, and sickness churned in my gut at Daria's voice. I wanted to vomit all over her as she strolled past me in her tiny skirt and heels, long legs so perfect.

My heart constricted, and a savage rage flared within me. The urge to attack her grew by the second...

"There you are. Why are you wasting your time with this rodent?" she whined, sparing me the barest of glances from the corner of her eye before she wrapped herself practically around Wilder's arm. And instantly, that hardness in his face softened as he looked down at her.

I think at that moment, I felt the last fragment of my heart crack.

The enduring way he stared down at her ruined me. He was supposed to only look at me that way... only me!

Tears blurred my eyes, and I couldn't stand this a moment longer.

I whipped around and hurried away, my heartbeat thumping loudly in my ears while Daria's laughter boomed behind me.

Shoving past everyone, I rushed down the sidewalk, forgetting where I was going, but I needed to be as far from here as possible.

I inhaled each breath deeply and wiped away the tears, trying my best to force a semblance of calm over myself.

"They deserve each other," I kept whispering under my breath, even if I took the briefest glances over my shoulder to make sure they didn't follow me. "What am I doing? Can I live in a town with them like this?"

I wiped another loose tear when I heard someone calling my name. Of course, I flinched from the shiver zapping all the way down to my tailbone. I expected Daria to chase after me, to threaten me, to gloat. Anything that involved rubbing salt in my wounds.

When I looked back, she was nowhere to be seen.

"Rune," the voice came again, and I looked out across the main road to the other side where Miyu stood in the sun, wearing a red floral dress and waving at me to join her.

I blinked at her, convinced I was imagining this. My mind had finally broken and I was hallucinating things.

I didn't move at first, but glanced across the sidewalk behind me, uncertain if she was mocking me or maybe I misheard her calling my name.

But when she ushered me once more with a wide smile on her mouth, I swallowed the lump in my throat, wiped my eyes, and crossed the road, plucking the courage to find out where I stood with Miyu.

Her smile never faded when I stepped up onto the sidewalk to join her.

"Hi," I said wearily, then chewed on my lower lip.

"I've wanted to talk to you," she said instantly and took my hand in hers, guiding me towards the cafe behind her.

"Look, I'm sorry that things got out of control the other night," I explained, to which she smiled gently. Warmth gradually filled me to think that maybe my relationship with Miyu wasn't lost. What I desperately needed was a friend while so much around me fell apart.

She didn't respond but led me into the coffee shop.

The nutty aroma of coffee filled my nostrils the moment we stepped inside, followed by a sweet baking smell of cakes. The place was half full, and the owner, Mr. Jones was buzzing from one table to another serving drinks and pastries.

We moved to a small booth in the far corner, and I climbed in.

"Let me quickly order us some drinks, and then we can talk," she said and marched over to the counter before I could tell her what I wanted. Guess it was going to be a surprise.

I sat back, watching her chatting with Mr. Jones, who nodded at her order, then glanced up toward me and beamed a grin my way.

By the time Miyu returned and shuffled into the booth across the table from me, my nerves kicked in again. My entire body stilled, while my heart raced.

She reclined and exhaled loudly. "Things have been shit lately," she confessed. "And every day is a struggle, I'll be honest."

"I can only imagine." I pushed myself forward, watching her fidget with strands of her hair draped over her shoulder.

"The hardest parts are all the questions I have, and I don't know if I'll ever know the truth." Her lips pinched to the side, as though she fought the urge to cry. I wanted to move closer to her, to hold her, but I wouldn't push this. She wanted to talk, so I'd listen to her.

"We can keep trying every night to go to the town hall and see if Rae appears again."

The creases at the corners of her mouth deepened, and she gave no response. She didn't like my suggestion, so I kept quiet.

Just then, Mr. Jones arrived with our drinks. "Greetings. I have your drinks, Madams."

He placed a latte in front of me, then one for Miyu. He smiled at me with his blue eyes. As always, he had his well-pressed black suit on and a red apron wrapped around his waist. I loved how he always dressed so impeccably and resembled a mafia gangster boss with his black bowler hat.

"Thank you," I said, to which he gave a slight bow of his head, then he retreated and returned to fluttering around the room, collecting empty cups and welcoming new people entering the shop.

"Anyway, I wanted to make up with you," Miyu finally admits. "So, this is kind of a truce for the way I reacted. I never should have said those things to you. Can you forgive me?"

My chest rose and fell with the earlier warmth spreading through me at her words. I wanted to just hug her, and tears already pricked my eyes. I exhaled loudly and smiled. "Of course. I missed you so much." I stretched an arm across the table, and she took hold of my hand. "I'm always there for you. You mean the world to me."

Her eyes roved over her coffee, and she picked it up. "Here's to making things right." She raised her cup, the milky foam swishing across the top.

I breathed easier, my muscles relaxing as I picked up my cup. "To never letting anything get in the way of our friendship."

She grinned and took a long drink from her coffee, her eyes watching me.

And I did the same, part of me feeling like this was a sort of ritual moment that we'd remember when things strained between us. The coffee was hot, creamy, and so sweet. It rushed down my throat and seemed to awaken in me that happy part of me I'd suppressed with all the sorrowful emotions. "Oh, this is so good." I swallowed half of it, not realizing how thirsty I'd been.

"I can't tell you how much I needed this."

"The coffee is incredible here." She kept on sipping hers.

"Not that, but us, here, like this. It broke my heart to think I'd lost you as a friend."

"To be honest, I've never cried so much in my life as I have the last few days. And I could have used a friend, instead of pushing the one I had away."

I finished the coffee in no time, and Mr. Jones, as if on cue, replaced mine with a fresh cup, smiling at me, then returned to his work. The more I drank, the hotter I felt, and my pulse slowed down. I reclined, not remembering the last time I'd been so relaxed.

All my troubles were still in my mind, but somehow a simple coffee with a friend made everything bearable.

Miyu leaned forward, a smile curling on her lips. "How are you feeling?"

"Like I could fly," I answered with a laugh. "And if I'm being honest, I could easily eat half of the pastries on the counter."

All worries drifted from my mind. I couldn't recall the last time I'd felt so calm.

"Mr. Jones only has the best treats and coffees. But speaking of the truth, will you promise me to be honest from now on," she asked.

"Of course. Always." I took another mouthful of coffee, seriously eyeing the glass enclosure with pastries. I'd always had a weakness for sweet baked goodies, but I rarely had them while I lived with Alistair. They were for him and guests, and not for me as it would make me fat.

"Tell me, Rune, did you and Rae have an affair?"

I shook my head instantly, surprised she'd ask me that question again. "I told you last time. I would never."

She eyed me, tilting her head to the side. "Did you kiss him? Or maybe he kissed you while you were both at work?"

I huffed and held back the laughter so I didn't insult her. "Never. But you know who did once kiss me in the backroom when I first started working at the diner? Wilder. We broke a bottle of vodka in the process. We'd only barely just met, but I would have let him have sex with me at that moment. I was so turned on, and it was crazy." I take another sip of my coffee. "Geez, I've never told anyone that before. I don't want you to think I'm a nymphomaniac, but Daxon and Wilder bring something out of me, and let's just say we've had a lot of sex." I nod at her, lowering my voice.

She stared at me with a deadpan expression. "But what about Rae? You must have felt something for him. He's just as handsome, and so many girls wanted him when we first started dating."

"Nope, sorry. He's just not my type. I guess I like them big, growly, and possessive." I laughed at myself because I just described the kind of man I grew up thinking I'd never want to be with. Funny how fate worked.

Geez, why was I feeling so light-headed and relaxed at the same time?

Miyu huffed loudly, drawing Mr. Jones to our table. "Everything alright? Can I get you both anything else?"

"Cake," I suggested. "Maybe a selection plate. I don't even care about the calories right now."

"Okay, I'll bring you something nice." Then he turned to Miyu. "Everything seems to be fine here?"

Miyu nodded almost reluctantly. As Mr. Jones drifted away to the next table who called him, Miyu huffed again. "Why would Rae write about you in his journal?"

"Who knows. I mean, he was killing people in town, so I guess it was his serial killer notebook." The moment the words left my mouth, I regretted them. "Shit, I shouldn't have said it like that. I just feel so weird. I'm so sorry."

All the blood had drained from Miyu's face.

My stomach dropped at how thoughtless I'd been, bringing up Rae so carelessly. I clenched my jaw tight to shut the hell up, but the words burst past my mouth like I had no control of myself, like the desperate need to answer her trumped everything else.

"I'm sorry, Miyu. I still don't even understand how we never picked up on his scent at the murder scenes, but something was really wrong with him. I'm so sorry, babe."

"What the fuck, Rune," she said, raising her voice, drawing attention our way.

In my head, I was screaming at myself to keep my mouth shut. The agony crossing Miyu's face destroyed me, and all I could think was that she'd hate me forever now.

"Let's change topics quickly, please, because I feel strange." My knees bounced under the table. "Ducks. Did you know I saw some ducks in the river the other day?" I was rambling, needing to stop my mouth vomit.

Her gaze narrowed on me, her chin trembling. "Did you see him actually kill someone?" she asked with shaky words as tears drenched her cheeks.

I shuffled around the booth seat to reach her, to hug her. *Don't say a word. Don't you dare say a word.*

"Rune, stop. Just answer the fucking question."

A jolt of something zipped through me, and my response poured out of me like a raging river that no one could stop if they tried. And tears spilled from my eyes now too as the words flew out. "Daxon found Rae attacking someone in the woods, then he killed him."

I slapped a hand to my mouth, cursing myself. What the fuck was wrong with me?

A cry spilled from Miyu's lips. Her face was the color of a sheet of paper. She frantically scrambled to get out of the booth, her cries growing louder.

I lurched out of my seat, the room slightly spinning, and reached out for her. "Miyu, let me explain."

But she didn't listen and was already halfway across the coffee shop. Then she darted outside, vanishing from sight.

I crumbled in on myself and wanted to die at that moment. Wanted nothing more than to be hurt for what I'd done. Something was definitely wrong with me to have said all those things to her in such an insensitive way.

I stared down at the table, at my second coffee cup, empty, while Miyu barely touched her first one. Reaching over, I grabbed my cup and looked inside the remaining foam, then I sniffed it. The coffee was strong, and beneath it, something sweet lingered. Was that syrup or--

"Is everything alright? Where's Miyu?" Mr. Jones asked.

I raised my head, and his face was a blur behind my tears. Wiping my eyes, I noticed him staring at my coffee cup, and with that came the memory of the time he gave me a cup of his special tea mix that relaxed me.

An ache formed in my stomach, and it came from the reality that perhaps I was tricked.

"What did you put in my coffee?" I asked.

Mr. Jones' cheeks reddened and he wiped his hands on his apron. "What do you mean?"

"What. Did. You. Put. In. My. Coffee?" I asked again, louder this time, my entire body shaking violently.

He pursed his lips and bent over the table, whispering, "Miyu asked for my help. She just wanted to ask you a few questions, she said. It's not harmful, Rune, and will wear off in a couple of hours."

"You drugged me?" I gasped.

"It's a natural plant that encourages you to always tell the truth. I'm sorry." He pulled back, then returned to his counter.

My shoulders dropped, and the room tilted with me. I was going to be sick. I scrambled out of the booth and sprinted outside to the nearest trash can, where I hurled the contents of my stomach.

How could she have done this to me?

8

DAXON

I rounded the corner of my cabin, my eyes on my jeep, desperately needing to escape into the woods to get my fucking shit together, when I heard someone calling me from a distance.

Fuck! I wasn't in the mood for talking right now, unless it was to my girl, Rune.

And it definitely wasn't her voice.

My wolf growled from the disruption, hungry for the hunt, the rush of air in my fur, blood splashing on my face, my heart racing as I chased my prey.

When you had a monster living inside you, the trick came down to balance. I'd been so fucking uptight since killing Rae and Rune witnessing the whole ordeal, that I had to get my head together.

A sharp tug in my chest reminded me how much my precious Rune meant to me, how I made myself a promise to protect her. And it damn well destroyed me that I'd brought her agony by royally drawing her into my secrets.

Maybe it was for the best that she knew the true extent

of what I was capable of...after all, we were going to spend the rest of our lives together.

I enjoyed killing. It brought me exhilaration. I craved the rush of it, I loved watching my prey beg for mercy, their huge eyes pleading with me, the shock on their faces. I loved it all.

Never once had I felt regret or remorse for the people I eliminated. They all deserved what they got, so what was there to be sorrowful about?

It didn't bother me how long killings took either, and I'd be the first to admit that maybe I took too much enjoyment out of it. There was no rushing a fine piece of art.

Except, killing Rae left a distaste in my mouth. And it had fuck all to do with him not deserving what he got. But that Rune had to lay witness to the murder.

"Daxon," Miyu wailed from across the open field, stealing me out of my thoughts, her voice ringing loudly. When I glanced her way, several locals were staring too.

She marched toward me. And even from a distance, I saw the anger on her face, her arms wildly swinging by her side, the tears on her cheeks.

I let out a long breath. Well, fuck. Guess the cat was out of the bag about who killed Rae then. I should have spoken to her first instead of letting Rune drown with the knowledge and eventually cave by telling Miyu.

Nothing could be done about it now.

"H-how c-could you," Miyu stammered. Her face was red, and she looked stunned. Normally I wouldn't have bothered with silly little reassurances and platitudes like with time, she would learn to accept the decision...that she was fortunate he hadn't turned on her.

But the pain in her voice reached deep in my chest and

reminded me, she was a Bitten like me, one of my own, and her loss would impact the whole pack.

"I'm sorry, Miyu." I didn't apologize lightly, but I had murdered her mate. She deserved that at least.

She came at me without pause, her arm swinging wide, and her small fist clipped me across the face, the sting barely noticeable. My wolf snarled, shoving forward in defense. I lifted my gaze to the onlookers who expected me to deliver punishment for her strike.

Miyu hadn't done anything wrong though, and even I couldn't strike back with her in this state.

"You fucking bastard," she howled. "He was my husband, you psychopath. He loved me. He was my world." Holding her head high, she struggled to stop crying, her chest heaving for breath as she stood in front of me trembling. Even at her petite size, she didn't back down.

But grief had a way of making you feel like nothing could hurt you when you were drowning in unbearable pain.

"Come with me," I growled, seizing her arm and dragging her inside my cabin to leave behind the pack members not keeping to their own business.

"Rae has never hurt anyone," she cried, struggling to accept that her husband was a killer. "Why did you have to kill him? You could have kept him alive, let me talk to him."

I released her arm, and she stumbled backward before bumping into the back of my couch.

Staring down at my hands, I saw flashing blood in my mind, Rae's fury, and how I'd taken his life before he took Rune's. How I'd do it in a heartbeat again without hesitation. Then I glanced up to Miyu who had wild hair and heartbreak in her eyes.

"I can't guarantee you that things will be okay, Miyu.

Rae took three lives. Three families are still grieving for what he stole from them. Those are moments I can't bring back to them. And I hate that you're suffering, but Rae was not a good person. I wish I could take your hurt away. What he did is a shock to all of us. But I explained all this to you before. "

Shaking, she was crying loudly, her face buried in her hands.

"B-but i-its not like him. He wouldn't hurt anyone. It doesn't make any sense."

I took her into my arms, but she pushed against me, and I let her pummel her fists against my chest if it helped her get the anger out.

"One day you'll find your happiness again. A life filled with love."

I felt like a liar just saying the words. I knew how rare it was to find something special.

Instead of responding, she collapsed against me, crying hysterically.

I lifted her off her feet and put her down in the chair at my table, then I grabbed a bottle of cold water from the fridge and set it in front of her.

Silence stretched between us for a long time, until she finally fell quiet. She wiped her eyes and looked at me. Her skin was red and blotchy from how much she rubbed her cheeks. Her puffy eyes stared at me.

"I will never be okay with this because, in my heart, the Rae I know would never kill anyone. And instead of murdering him, you should have let me talk to him first. Because now, I'll always live with a hole in my heart."

What could I say to that? "I understand. And as your Alpha, I did what I needed to protect my pack. If I didn't, he would have taken another life." Mentioning that the life was Rune's wasn't going to help the situation or the strain between the two friends. "I will stay with you for as long as you need, help you through this, Miyu. And I promise you that slowly you will find light in the dark once more."

She sniffled. "I highly doubt that." Her words came out harsh, breathless, then she pushed to her feet and marched out of my cabin. She banged the door shut behind her.

I took a deep breath, then climbed to my feet. "For fuck's sake." I headed out of the cabin and straight into the woods, tearing my clothes off me. My wolf poured out of me. I hit the ground with my paws and howled, piercing the silence. Birds burst out from nearby trees, flying away. And me, I lunged into the forest, needing to kill something.

———

Rune

Cold air rushed across my back and through my hair as I stumbled down the sidewalk. Tears refused to stay at bay while my chest hurt like someone had carved my heart out from right under my rib cage.

How could Miyu have drugged me? How could she think that was okay?

All my life I had been treated like crap, lied to, pushed around. Deciding to live in Amarok came with the promise that I'd left that life behind. And yet lately, everything went against the idyllic lifestyle I hoped for.

And those I considered close to me ended up hurting me the most. It was cruel, and their actions twisted my insides into a horrible mess. I wanted to run from town and leave it all behind... make a clean break for it. After all, I'd done it once, why not again?

The promise of pain flared through me, and I knew it

wouldn't leave me if I ran. I hated that I'd let myself get close to so many people that I almost crumbled at the notion of abandoning them. Despite the horrible ache of seeing Wilder in that bitch's arms, having my best friend turn on me, and knowing that Daxon enjoyed killing people, I couldn't make myself leave either.

Clearly, something was definitely broken inside of me because it almost felt like I enjoyed being hurt.

After all, I should have been disgusted by Daxon's actions, but I wasn't. And that confused me. Instead, I found him brutally beautiful.

Not looking where I was going, I wiped my eyes and walked right into someone... more like a wall of muscle. I bounced back, blinking my eyes as I raised my head to the man towering in front of me. The first thing I saw was piercing deep blue eyes that reminded me of a moonless night.

"Careful there, little one," Ares said, his voice smooth, feeling like silk running over my skin. His head tilted to the side as he studied me, his lips pulling into a spectacular smile.

"I'm sorry, I wasn't looking where I was going," I said, my stomach buzzing with butterflies. "Seems I'm making a habit of running into you." I found myself grinning. I barely knew this man, but I couldn't help but be charmed by the soft expression on his face and the mischievous light in his eyes.

Dressed in a black button-up shirt that sat open at his throat and jeans, he was incredibly handsome.

My heart raced as his gaze gently fell to my mouth.

"Are you okay?" he asked genuinely.

I nodded, not even sure how I'd explain my life to a complete stranger. Plus, part of me wanted him to think I was normal, for as long as possible. There was something relaxing about him not knowing my past. It meant I could pretend to be someone in control of my life.

Dark and tall, Ares reached over and pulled a leaf out of my hair, looking at me with a curious expression. I breathed in his heady scent on the breeze. It was masculine, sweet, and pungent, which was a strange, alluring combination.

"I seem to have an unfair advantage that you seem to always catch me off guard," he said. "Anyway, you're in a rush to get somewhere again?"

I raised an eyebrow, recalling the first time I almost knocked him over. I had been hurrying into the inn to avoid crossing paths with Wilder.

I shrugged. "It's been a crazy week, or more like a few months, in all honesty."

Just then, two young women strolled past us on the sidewalk, their gazes wide and on Ares. They whispered in a way they hoped would steal his attention.

Ares looked over to them and winked, the small gesture sending them into a giggle, and both blushed as they kept glancing over their shoulder at him.

"You've got yourself a small fan club," I teased.

"They're just curious," he answered nonchalantly. Ares' smile was contagious, and under his gaze, it felt like the rest of the world faded away.

His brow pinched lightly. "What's your name? I meant to ask you last time we met."

"Rune," I answered, then nibbled on my lower lip.

"Rune," he repeated, breathing my name like it was a whisper in my ear. "Beautiful name."

He stared at me like nothing else could hold his interest more, and to say my eyes weren't glued to him would be a terrible lie. From the blue hue in his dark hair to a face that was all sharp angles, to his thick biceps and a body that could easily sweep me off my feet, I fluttered my eyes at his compliment.

I shouldn't be picturing him as anything other than a stranger I passed on the street, yet something about him made me want to remain in his company.

"What brings you into Amarok?" I asked. "I haven't seen you before."

"Would you believe me if I said I'm sightseeing?"

"Nope," I replied quickly. "No one comes to Amarok without a reason to be here." I gave him a lopsided smirk, enjoying him not knowing that I was a stranger here too.

He laughed, making a deliciously warm sound. "The truth is quite a dull story. Nothing that exciting."

"Then I definitely want to hear it," I answered, caught up in how calm I seemed around him, enjoying the peace from all the crazy in my life of late.

"Come, walk with me," he said, and without a reason not to, I joined him. "For the past five years, I was in the army. I was just recently discharged, so I decided to explore and see more of the country. Been driving for a few days, and I sort of just ended up in this town." He stared ahead, the sun on his face. "And I like it here, so I'm staying for a few days. Told you, pretty boring."

"This town does have that magnetic pull, as I ended up here very similarly," I admitted. I frowned when I realized that the man might not be a wolf shifter at all, but perhaps a normal human who'd found himself in the town.

The few humans I had met while living with Alistair always appeared scared, though. Ares was the complete opposite. He walked in a strange town with confidence, like he was untouchable. Even the people we passed watched him, almost enthralled by his presence. He was beautiful when he moved, so graceful and powerful, drawing my attention to his muscular body, how tall he stood. I had no clue who Ares was, but I was curious to find out.

Strolling with him flooded me with forbidden excitement. He didn't know a thing about me, and it was delightful to have no judgment at all. I wanted us to be just normal strangers talking about normal things. As much as one can be normal in a secret wolf town.

"Do you believe in fate, Rune?" he asked, his voice lulling me out of my thoughts.

I wanted to think of a witty response, but my head was still in a whirlwind from what had happened with Miyu, so I went with honesty. "I was brought up to believe fate was set and would look after you. But apparently, fate forgot about the latter when it came to me. So, it's hard to believe in something that has constantly let me down."

He ran a hand through his dark hair, the soft curls bouncing around his face. "I believe fate isn't always going to give us the happily ever after we all dream of."

"True, but I would have loved a few good vibes coming my way." I half laughed, while part of me sighed internally at how true that was.

His deep, blue eyes flashed my way, then he turned down a side street that took us past the grocery store.

I guessed he wanted me to follow, which I did, and he waited for me to catch up. "Everything happens for a reason." He dragged the back of his hand across his mouth, staring at me with a hunger I hadn't seen earlier, and it didn't scare me. It called me to him. "Don't you ever feel that when something happens, or you meet someone, and everything in your mind just clicks like this feels right?"

The confidence in his voice gave credence to his words and almost had me accepting them as the truth. Except, I'd felt that same feeling he mentioned with two men, and look how that ended.

"All I know is that I'm not happy with whoever is in charge of my fate up to now," I responded with a half-grin.

The corners of his ridiculously sexy mouth curled upward.

And all the while, with us walking side by side, his arm brushing against mine, it ignited a burning ache in the pit of my stomach.

What was wrong with me? Couldn't I meet a gorgeous man and not keep my emotions normal and well away from anything sexy?

We passed the grocery store where several people glanced our way, studying the newcomer. An older man even tipped his hat at Ares. I couldn't help but wonder if Ares had been in town before for them to be so welcoming of him.

When the man glanced at me, his nose wrinkled, like my presence upset him.

What the hell? They didn't even know Ares and were kinder to him than me.

"Why is everyone being so nice to you?" I said abruptly, realizing I'd voiced my thoughts. It came out a bit more intense than I'd intended to.

Ares laughed again, the sound soothing, and somehow it took the edge off. And no one seemed to be acting crazy around him, which was a welcome breath of fresh air.

"People are naturally drawn to me," he explained like this was a normal occurrence.

"Lucky you," I murmured.

At the end of the street, we emerged into a small park where several locals were by the river, feeding wild ducks. A worn path snaked along the river, trees dotting the land spaciously. There were even several benches in the place. I needed to visit here more often, it was incredibly tranquil.

"How long have you lived here?" he asked.

"It's been around four months, though some days it feels like it's only been weeks with so much happening. The town is wonderful, and the locals are...interesting, so you'll enjoy your visit. Where are you staying?"

We walked several feet before he responded, "I'm staying in—"

A thunderous growl came from behind us, stealing his words.

I flinched instantly. Ares' arm snapped around my back, drawing me to his side protectively.

"Rune!" Daxon's dark voice sliced through the air, and my calm heart jumped. It slammed into my ribcage, and I spun, knowing exactly what Daxon would think. What he was capable of. My world wobbled around me.

Dread spread through me like wildfire, and all I could think was that Daxon was going to murder Ares. I snapped around to face him, moving away from Ares' hold, needing to diffuse the situation.

Daxon's shoulders were bunched up, his mouth open, the whites of his eyes visible like the sight of seeing me with Ares rendered him startled. And his sights were set on Ares.

Panic tasted like bile at the back of my throat.

He came toward us in long strides, his eyes narrowing, hands fisted by his side. This was so fucking bad.

My gaze darted back to Ares, who stared at Daxon, almost oblivious. Then I stared back at the man I loved who I was learning more every day was a savage force of nature.

He'd kill this poor man who had done nothing wrong.

Images of Rae popped into my mind, of how easily Daxon had killed him, and fear flooded me.

"Daxon, stop, please," I called out, shoving myself in front of him, needing him to stop.

But he moved too fast, and where one minute he was coming in my direction, the next, he'd sidestepped past and flew at Ares. The buffet of air from his movement rocked into me, and the rumble of growls and hissing filled the air.

I whipped around, a cry on my throat. "Daxon, stop."

The two clashed. I kept expecting Ares to fall, to have Daxon slamming his fists into him, but it never happened. Ares moved like the wind, sidestepping, ducking, leaping out of the way of every blow Daxon delivered.

They swept across the park, crashing into trees, tossing each other, but they kept getting back up. I dragged my feet after them, terrified this was going to end tragically, but also completely confused by what I was seeing.

The strikes Daxon managed to get in did nothing to Ares. He took them easily. What the hell was he?

Never in a million years would I have expected to see Daxon flying backward as Ares tossed him away like he weighed nothing.

I gasped in utter shock.

Frozen on my feet as if they took root into the ground, I watched Ares straighten his torn shirt and stuff his hands into his pockets. He strolled toward me and winked, despite the gash across his cheek. The same one where blood dripped over his jawline. Right before my eyes, the wound knitted back together, healing.

What the fuck!

"You better tend to your boyfriend," he said with that soothing voice, sending a wave of calm through me, which now kind of scared me. "I'll be seeing you around, Rune."

"W-what are you?"

He chuckled once more, and just like that he sauntered back into town, vanishing into the gathering crowd near the street. They parted for him like he was a god.

Daxon was seething as he leapt to his feet, his gaze scanning the park.

"Where the fuck did he go?" he growled, storming toward me. Blood seeped from the cut under his eye. More red trickled from the gash on his neck. He blinked at the street, then back at me.

His lips thinned, his arms shaking at his sides. I'd never seen anyone get the upper hand against Daxon. Except for Wilder, but even then, they were two tanks locked into an endless match.

But what I'd just witnessed left me staring at Daxon incredulously. My mind barely caught up with what I'd seen, but it was clear I'd been wrong. Ares was definitely not human. He couldn't be... But I also couldn't smell wolf on him.

"I don't think he intends to harm anyone. Why would you attack him?"

His gaze locked with mine, and he frowned at my question.

"That asshole is dead," he snarled, but instead of giving chase, he embraced me, then studied my face as if checking for bruises. "Did he hurt you?"

"No, we were just talking." With my thumb, I wiped the blood rolling down his cheek. Seeing him hurt squeezed my chest. Despite all the crap going on, I'd given Daxon my heart, and I loved him. "Do you know what he is then?"

He shook his head, the cords in the column of his neck flexing. "I couldn't tell," he muttered under his breath.

Then he glanced down at me, his arms holding onto my waist, his fingers digging into my flesh.

His voice sounded almost brittle, the struggle on his face twisting his features. Daxon wasn't a man who lost often, and it rattled him.

"D-do you think he could be a hybrid wolf hunter?" A shiver raced up my spine.

"Doubt it, or he would have killed you already. Plus he smells differently than they usually do. What were you doing with him though? Why would you let him touch you?" that dark, jealous voice returned, and his hold constricted around me.

My world was still spinning from how fast a casual walk had turned into a chaotic storm, but Daxon's words pulled me out of my mind. And I pushed myself out of his embrace, not ready to deal with his jealousy right now.

"You don't need to go crazy every time I speak with a guy," I said, retreating and moving quickly into the park.

Heavy footfalls closed in behind me, and I turned just as Daxon locked his arms around me, turning me on the spot, his mouth crashing against mine.

"No, you're not running from me again," he breathed against my mouth. "You've had your time." Then he kissed me again with such fervor that I knew instantly that any attempt I made to walk away from him would ruin me.

9

DAXON

I could never get enough of Rune. She was my obsession, my addiction, my everything. And to have another man dare to touch her left me seething.

Motherfucker! My insides burned just from knowing some asshole had dared to touch my girl.

She was mine, mine, mine!

Her body softened against me as I kissed her deeply and tried to remind her that she belonged to me. Fuck, she was just too beautiful to be real, and it drove me insane to have her pissed at me. I knew she hadn't forgiven me yet, but I'd given her enough time to get over it. This was happening.

Fire leapt off her body and onto mine, her back arching, those gorgeous breasts crushed against my chest.

The breeze swished past us, reminding me we were in the park, but I wanted her, now.

She broke away from me, gasping for air, while a growl kindled in my throat.

Lust stirred in her gaze, her nipples pushing tight against the fabric of her white dress. I tried to pull her closer, but she recoiled. "Rune," I warned.

"I'm not weak," she said, her head high.

"I never said you were." My intention wasn't to scare her, but I was also a man who took what he wanted.

"You attacked Ares when he did nothing wrong. It was terrifying, Daxon."

Whatever the hell had happened during our fight took me by surprise. And that meant a lot because no one could stand head to head against me, except Wilder. And, well, he'd got himself royally screwed and lost right now so he wasn't a threat.

Wilder may have taken himself out of the running, but I sure as fuck wasn't going to allow another bastard to make his move on my girl.

He got a lucky break, but next time he wouldn't see me coming.

I also wasn't a complete moron though. Whoever that dick was, he wasn't a wolf, but he had unimaginable strength. And no one with that kind of power randomly walked into Amarok. They came with purpose... What his purpose was, I didn't care. I just wanted him gone.

Rune might not see it, but no guy wanted to just be her friend without benefits. It was how our sex-driven minds worked. The moment any of us saw a beauty like my sweetheart, only one thing crossed our minds. Getting a chance to rut her. We were wired that way... to fuck females and fight for our right to do so. I'd fallen in love with her hard, and I'd fight to the death to keep her safe and mine.

We may live in a modern world, but at the heart of it, wolf shifters were primal, savage beasts who wanted two things.

To hunt prey.

And fuck females.

"I've tried really hard to be calm and give you the time

you need, but that ends now. You're spending your nights with me from now on. And forget that asshole, Ares. I'll take care of him."

"Daxon," she pleaded. "No more killing. Please."

Leaning toward me, the desperation in her eyes had my heart squeezing. "If you asked me, I'd give you the stars from the sky." I cupped the sides of her face. "When you're away from me, I'm a fucking mess and I need you by my side."

Something clicked into place for me from the moment I saw Rune, and I wasn't going to lose her.

"Promise me," she said, her lips pinching. "I want to hear it."

"I give you my word I will try my best to not kill him."

"Daxon." She sighed.

Drawing her closer, I kissed her lightly. "I'm being honest with you. When someone touches anything that's mine, I won't forget it. But for you, I will try. I just ask that you stay away from him until I work out what he's really doing in town."

She nodded, and her fingers ran a trail along my neck and brushed through my hair where she wound the short strands around her fingers. Her touch was hypnotic.

Despite her actions, she frowned, her brow pinching with annoyance. She fought her own attraction. Even when she was mad at me, I couldn't help but admire how absolutely stunning she was, and lust rocked through me.

Doubt danced on her face, and before she could give me another reason or excuse that she needed more time, that she had every right to talk to anyone she chose, I kissed those adorable lips. Dragging my mouth to her ear, I whispered, "I want you naked, my tongue flicking your nipples, my cock inside you. I can tell you want me too."

Her moan drove me wild. My cock hardened, bulging in my pants, my need growing.

I glanced over my shoulder to the couple by the river, with their backs to us. I had no doubt they were eavesdropping.

I gave a whistle, which made them glance our way, the man's eyes wide.

"Leave," I demanded, to which he and his girl made a hasty retreat toward town. I grabbed Rune's hand and drew her to the private part of the park where trees were denser, where a wooden bench called to me.

She glanced back toward town, but I didn't give a fuck if anyone saw us. "Take your underwear off," I instructed her.

Her breaths sped up, and she hesitated at first.

"Either you do it, or I tear them off." I stepped toward her, and she narrowed her gaze. "Show me your breasts."

A feisty expression flared over her face, and it looked gorgeous on her. I loved seeing her come out of her shell that her ex had pushed her into.

She slid her hands under her dress, jiggled about, and slid her underwear down her legs.

"How about you show me your cock?" she countered, throwing her underwear at me angrily.

I laughed out loud that she'd think that was any kind of punishment. I snatched her panties out of the air and pressed them to my nose. Inhaling deeply, I let her heady scent drown me, to fill every inch of me. All I wanted was to think of her.

"Fuck me, you smell delicious." My balls felt heavy, my dick aching to release. Tucking the underwear into my pocket, I grabbed her wrist. "Come here, you're too far."

She stumbled near and our bodies collided. Then I kissed her hard so she'd remember her place, all while walking us to the bench. I fisted her hair behind her head to hold her in place, my hand on her breast, squeezing. I tore the fabric of her dress, wrenching it down with her bra to expose the most beautiful breasts.

Taking a seat, I lowered my mouth to pink, pebbled nipples, and drew one into my mouth. She heaved a shuddering cry, her hands were in my hair, and I ran a hand up the insides of her legs.

Fire scorched my hand, her arousal drenching her inner thighs. Taking the second nipple between my teeth, I flicked it with my tongue.

With my fingers, I parted her lips and pressed a thumb to her clit, rubbing it in slow circles, wanting her to beg me.

She slackened into me, moaning, and I tugged on her nipple then flicked it.

My need thundered through me, my balls so fucking tight, and with my free hand, I unzipped my jeans. My cock sprung out, and I snarled from the freedom, from the urgency to plunge into her wet pussy.

"Sit on me, baby," I said, drawing her toward me with my hold on her pussy.

She smiled deviously and raised her dress to show me her glistening, shaved pussy.

I palmed my cock a few times, the tip covered in precum. I loved seeing her naked.

"Is this what you want?" she asked on a shuddering breath.

I was loving this new side of her. So, I handed her the reins and lounged on the bench, arms stretched out on either side of me. "I'm all yours, sweetheart."

Her gaze lowered to my cock sitting upright and waiting for her. Then she climbed on top of me, straddling me. The petite thing barely weighed a thing, but the impact she had on me was earth-shattering.

Heat flooded me as she lowered that gorgeous pussy over me, sliding over my cock with her slick, teasing me.

I grinned at the way she liked to play with me, but she had no clue that I was the wolf about to devour her. For now, I let her have her fun.

She leaned in, and her tongue swept across my lips just as she pushed herself over my cock. I hissed, my hands gripping the bench, and the little minx bit my lower lip. The pain pinched just as she sat down completely over me. I growled while she purred like a cat.

I kissed her, but she pulled back, smirking. When I leaned forward, she placed her palm on my chest. "We're doing this my way."

Who was I to complain... "Then fuck me." I licked my lips, tasting the metal from the cut on my tongue.

With her hands gripping my shoulders and her tits in my face, she started to rock that tight little pussy over my dick. Her smell filled me, and the soft sounds she made as she rode me made me want to sink my teeth into her.

But I gave her what she wanted... I sat back, my body on a high from how well my bunny bounced up and down on me. It felt incredible to have her small body possessing me, her cunt gripping my cock, and eyes on me.

Her spectacular perky breasts bounced, and my gaze followed their delicate curves, the hardened tips, her white hair fluttering behind her in the breeze. The smooth skin I craved to lick.

She was a goddess, and I loved seeing the sweat sheen on her brow, her eyes so lustful. I wondered how close she was to coming. "It feels so good," she murmured, her fingernails digging into my shoulders with delicious pain.

Her hips twitched with each plunge, and her eyes fluttered upward.

Screw waiting any longer. I loved how she fucked me, but I needed to plow into her, to slam so hard that my name tainted those luscious, full lips.

I grasped her hips and lifted us both up off the bench, my cock still fully impaled in her. Her gasp made me smile.

"My turn, pet." I pulled her off me, much to her protesting groan.

"Hey, that wasn't part of the deal." Despite her words, they were breathy, and she was close to an orgasm.

"I want it my way now." I guided her to face away from me and slid my hand up her back, forcing her to bend over the bench. I bunched up her dress, pushing it up and over her ass, exposing her. "I suggest you hold on. I'm about to fuck you hard."

My chance to see it all left me loving every second of her bare ass in the air, her wet pussy on display. I ran a finger from her drenched slit to her asscrack, and I slid a finger into her ass. She tensed, but she was so turned on, so wet, that her body welcomed my invasion.

When she glanced over her shoulder at me, her huge eyes filled with wonder.

"Is this what you want?" I asked.

She chewed on her lower lip, and nodded.

I ran the tip of my cock across her slickness, and while she tried to shift out of the way, I pressed the tip into her ass. "Right here, Rune?"

"Yes, Daxon," she breathed out, her hips bucking to meet my cock.

Fuck, she was tight, but the sensation was bliss. Seductive, all-consuming bliss that flooded every inch of my body as I fucked her ass.

Her moans deepened the faster I claimed her. She writhed beneath me, and I drew in ragged breaths with how hard she sucked on my cock, squeezing it. My hips moved, finding a rhythm, and I needed her to come. I needed her to not forget every time I'd fucked her, and to want more of me, crave me.

The primal urge flared through me, and I would never tire of touching her.

"Fuck, that's so good," she moaned, and I reached around her waist, my fingers sliding over her clit.

Continuing to rub, I thrust deeper into her, giving her every single inch I had until she cried out my name.

I growled as I claimed her, and my sweetheart gave herself to me willingly.

Her moans morphed into a beautiful scream with my name on her lips, her body shuddering. She came apart under me, my own explosion ripping through me. Snarling, I thrust one last time into her, flooding her with my seed.

My eyes rolled back, the world sinking away, and only we existed at that moment. It wasn't long before I pulled out of her and collected her into my arms. I held her tight as I took a seat on the bench with my gorgeous soon to be mate in my arms. She was breathing heavily, too dazed to speak, but her eyes smiled with her satisfaction.

She sank into my arms, and I held her, kissing her brow. My pulse thumped in my veins. I couldn't imagine my life without her.

"You've caged my heart, Rune," I cooed. "And I'll walk into fire with my eyes open, let the world see me come undone, anything so long as I don't lose you."

"I love you too," she whispered in a rushed breath. "I always will."

Rune

I moved through the main street of Amarok in the middle of the night as though I floated on the wind. Silence surrounded me, and I kept on walking quickly like I had to be somewhere, I just couldn't recall where. Time flashed, and one moment I was on the sidewalk, the next everything went dark.

With a startled jolt, I flipped open my eyes to find myself stumbling in the middle of the woods. My heart hammered in my chest, with a cry spilling past my lips.

"No, not again." I'd been sleepwalking right out of Daxon's cabin. And he had no clue or he'd be here with me.

Crap. Why did I have to end up in the forest of all places? I was getting really tired of this.

Of course, my mind flew to the monster in the forest, and I spun on the spot, trying to see the lights from the town. Anything to give me direction.

I shivered, and hugged myself, discovering I was barefoot when I stepped on a sharp pebble. Plus, wearing my pajama pants and thin tee was not conducive to being lost in the woods.

Darkness seemed to press in around me quickly, the breeze rustling the trees, and an owl hooted somewhere in the distance. I rubbed the goosebumps from my arms, and dread crept up my spine.

"There's nothing here to hurt me," I murmured under my breath, repeating it, and decided to move because I wouldn't find a way back home standing still.

Taking careful steps across the ground covered in twigs and dead leaves, I kept scanning the area when finally I spotted several blinking lights in the distance.

I could have cheered out loud, but I also didn't want to make too much noise. Hurrying forward, I kept watching the ground so I didn't step on a snake or something.

Suddenly, the lights vanished, and I paused with confusion. Then something blurred out of the way, revealing the lights once more... And the truth of what I'd just seen rattled me to my bones.

Someone else was in the woods with me.

Fuck, please don't let it be the monster.

Something big enough to blot out my view would not be a bunny rabbit.

My stomach churned, and there was no way I could hold back my control then. I screamed, hating how much I shook, then I backed up into a tree.

The monster. It's all I could think about. I was running to my left, in the opposite direction I'd seen the figure move.

Fear tightened my chest. I wanted to keep screaming while fear pummelled into me. With all these murders in town, it'd be my luck that I ended up as the next victim, and then everyone would see that Rae wasn't the murderer. But at my cost!

I rushed, branches whacking me in the face, shrubs tearing at my clothes, and I didn't stop. Even when I stepped on every damn sharp thing in this forest.

I kept looking over my shoulder.

Just then, the dark blur flashed across the path I'd just carved through the woods. And as it did, I tripped. That time, my cry rushed out.

Before I even hit the ground, my death flashed in my mind. With my hip hitting a gnarled root sticking out of the ground, I winced. Lifting my head, I looked back to where I'd seen the figure.

Everything was happening too quickly. I trembled so hard it felt like my heart was pounding its way through my ribcage. Darkness reached out for me with claws, tearing through me, keeping me prisoner to the fear shuddering in my bones.

And there it was. A creature as dark as the night on all fours, snorting. Hot breath floated from the corners of its dog-like mouth. Except, this was no dog or wolf. How could it be when it reached at least seven-foot on all fours and had razor spikes running down its spine.

Red eyes narrowed on me.

Goddess, I was going to die.

I called to my wolf, needing to not be the victim, but to fight back if this was going to be my end. She surged forward, the pressure across my body so intense that I felt her resistance. I felt my head spin.

Something warm trickled from my nose, and I wiped it away, knowing it was blood before I even looked at my fingers. What was wrong with my wolf?

The creature's nostrils flared as it stalked toward me.

Panicked, I dragged myself backward on my ass, my hand patting the ground for a weapon, anything to help me.

It drew in a sharp inhale, most likely taking in my scent... and the blood from my nose. I was so stupid... talk about serving myself up as a meal to a starved monster.

I scrambled to my feet, clutching in my hand a broken branch. The beast came closer, and the ground beneath me seemed to slip with how hard I shook. My fingers tightened around my weapon, and I knew this was my time to sink or swim.

Running wasn't an option. My wolf wouldn't come out,

but at the heart, I was still a wolf. And I'd not die out here like this.

"Get away," I called out with a shaky voice, lifting my weapon.

Never show fear to a predator.

Never run.

Always appear bigger than you were.

I had no choice now but to survive.

A terrifying growl came from behind me, and I shuddered, spinning so fast that I stumbled on my feet from how quickly the world spun with me.

Please don't let it be another creature ready to fight over who gets to eat me.

Strong arms caught me, and I cried out, swinging the branch in my hand at the new beast.

"It's me," he said, catching the wrist of my arm. "You're safe."

The sound of my pulse thrashing in my ears escalated. "Ares?" I gasped, then swung back around to find the creature gone.

"There's a monster in these woods," I cried. "It was just about to attack me."

"It's a wild animal, and it's gone," he reassured me, brushing my hair off my face.

My panic had stolen my breath, and I jumped when the damn owl hooted again.

"What are you doing in the middle of the woods at this time of night, Rune?"

"I-I...was sleepwalking. It's been happening a bit lately. I don't know why." I checked over my shoulder again. "What was that thing?"

"Let's get you out of the woods. You must be freezing in such thin clothes," he said calmly, and I wasn't going to argue. I was freezing. With his hand across my lower back, we moved hastily through the woods. I kept glancing over my shoulder though. I was surprised Ares never did once. But I guess I had seen him fight. Maybe he thought he was the biggest monster in these woods.

The thought made me shiver even more.

"Thank you," I said softly.

Light pulsed amid the trees as we moved closer to town, and only once we stepped out of the forest could I breathe easily. It still didn't stop me from walking super fast to get the hell away from the woods.

We'd emerged right behind the town hall, and seriously, I was beginning to really dislike this place. Why did everything scary happen near the building?

Ares held me tight against his side, and I realized his body was cold. How long had he been outside? When I looked up at him, I could have sworn his eyes glinted red in the moonlight.

Then again, I might have been imagining it with my panic-induced brain because anything would make me jump at that moment.

Movement from the town hall window caught my attention, and I stared in that direction, finding nothing. I did, however, manage to hit a rock with my foot, which stung, and I tripped while cursing under my breath.

Ares' arm around my waist tightened, and he swooped me back onto my feet with ease.

"Look at you," Ares whispered in that perfect, soothing voice. "You're trembling, but I've got you."

It was a strange sensation to feel both terrified and weirdly turned on by this huge man who came out of nowhere like a knight in shining armor to save me. He wore all black, his hair wind-blown, and in the night, the blue hue in his hair appeared more pronounced. He was absolutely gorgeous.

"What were *you* doing in the woods?" I asked.

He studied me with those dark eyes, standing tall beside me. And so close that his scent filled me--slightly earthy and potently male. A zip of electricity ran across my skin.

"Couldn't sleep," he answered, then lifted his hand to my face. His touch was smooth like he'd never done hard labor with his hands, unlike Daxon who had a bit more of a callused feel. "I've always had trouble sleeping. Too much on my mind."

"Oh, I know that feeling," I responded. "I'm surprised I actually get to sleep most nights." My attempt to force a laugh came out sounding like a strangled choke.

"I once joked that I was a person who needed to do a lot of things, but in truth, I am trapped in a body that wants to sleep all the time."

That time I giggled for real. "You might have just described me. So, is that why you're wandering in the woods aimlessly?"

"It was your scream that drew me into the forest. I was just making my way to the bar to see if they'd still be open at this ungodly hour."

"Sounds like good timing to me," I answered. "Seriously, I might have died out there without your help. Whatever is out there, it's not a normal animal."

"The night can also make things appear a lot scarier than they are," he said. "But I used to sleepwalk," he admitted. "A long time ago though. This one time I woke up on the edge of a cliff. It was the most terrifying thing."

"Crap. I really hope I don't do that, or I'll probably tumble over the edge from fright."

"Thankfully, I stumbled backward, but after that night, I tried everything. Locking my doors and windows from the outside, tying myself to the bed with rope, having someone watch over me. But nothing worked. I always found a way back to the damn cliff's edge."

I studied the way he spoke, how the corners of his mouth pinched. "So, how did you stop it?"

He shrugged. "I went to the cliff during the day and stood there, trying to work out why it kept calling me."

"And?" Captivated by his every word, I hadn't even noticed we'd been slowly tracking our way toward the bridge.

"And, well, I realized as I stood up there, staring out over the wide expanse of the forest, how little I enjoyed my life. And that maybe leaping off the edge would solve everything. I guess my sleepwalking was following my subconscious." He blinked into the distance, his chin high, and shadows crowded under his eyes as if the pain remained raw in his mind.

My heart squeezed at hearing his ache.

I reached out and touched his arm. "Well, I'm glad you didn't jump and that you're here."

I offered him a smile when he glanced my way, but the look on his face remained haunted. The weak grin he gave me troubled me. "Yes, something like that," he responded, like there was so much more to this story than he was willing to share.

And just as quick as his solemn expression appeared, a new look washed over his face... the confident one where nothing in the world could touch him.

Ares' hand on my cheek pulled me closer to him instantly, like his voice held power over me. And under his gaze, my heart caught on fire from his wicked grin.

"Who are you exactly?" I whispered as the events from earlier in the day came to mind. His fight with Daxon flashed in my thoughts, along with how easily Ares deflected his attacks.

"I am only a shadow," he answered, his thumb stroking my cheek. "And you, my dear Rune, are the light. Too much light for this town."

I swallowed hard as my stomach filled with butterflies. I grew hot and tingly all over, completely forgetting what I'd just said. When I looked into his eyes, I forgot myself, and the world fell into the abyss. Somehow, the smallest touch and words from him rendered me hopelessly lost.

I knew very well what desire felt like. How it left me yearning with need, pining for the man who simply looked at me a certain way, touched me lightly, and had my body burning up. I'd only felt that sensation with two men... Wilder and Daxon.

Until now... Until Ares.

"Some call me a monster, but it's very subjective, isn't it? Just like this town of wolves... to humans we are all monsters," he whispered, his upper lips peeling back over white, sharp teeth.

I should have been scared, I knew this, and yet I also wanted everything he offered in his gaze. My world was made of straw in comparison, and he was about to burn it all down...

And with each passing second, my head grew fuzzier.

His thumb continued to stroke my cheek, while his other hand fell to my waist, making a trail to the middle of my back where he held me firmly against him.

Our gazes locked, and the world seemed to freeze around us. My heartbeat thumped in my chest cavity. And then he leaned in toward me. His soft, supple lips pressed against mine, and their tenderness surprised me. He tasted like whiskey, something metallic, and a lingering sweetness. Everything about his taste in my mouth left me craving more.

But it was happening too fast, and I quickly pulled away from him, stepping out of his arms. Heat seared across my face at his kiss.

He straightened back, looking at me with genuine concern painted on his face. "Rune, I'm sorry. I never should have kissed you."

"I-I'm taken. I can't do this." I recoiled and turned to leave because I shouldn't be having any kind of feelings for Ares. I had Daxon and whatever tangled mess existed with Wilder.

But as I started to run, my pulse racing rampant, Ares grabbed my arm and brought me to a stop.

"I'm not going to let you run off in the night alone. Let me walk you back safely."

Pausing, I turned toward him, and it was crazy that each time I looked into his eyes, something inside me made me feel calm and told me I'd be safe with him.

"Come to me," he said, his voice so alluring that my legs moved of their own accord, like my body belonged to him.

My wolf growled in my chest to leave, yet I couldn't make myself divert from the path I'd set towards Ares.

I gasped, yet my mind was fighting me. His very presence seemed to suck the soul right out of me.

"Don't resist me," he said quietly, and my body softened. My ability to think vanished, replaced with his manly scent, with the way his muscular body felt against mine, how suddenly good his lips felt on my neck. I pressed my breasts against his chest and moaned while holding onto his shirt.

"Ares," I breathed his name, both perplexed and burning up.

"I'm right here," he moaned with a deep voice that didn't sound like him. But when his mouth fell back to the curve of my neck, I melted.

The stinging bite of teeth scraped across on my skin, then pierced flesh, igniting a fire that raced through me, diving all the way to the carnal pleasures deep in the pit of my stomach. My knees wobbled, and I cried out from the delicious pain while holding onto him. The soothing stroke of his tongue across the bite mark drove me crazy, and I couldn't hold back the moans.

"I've wanted you from the first time I laid eyes on you," he said. "I'd been watching you for a while." His teeth pierced my skin once more, and exhilaration thrummed through me, my thighs pressing together. I was soaking wet. The muscles deep inside me pulsed with desperation for him to claim me, but the more he sucked and licked my neck, the more my body screamed for him.

Whatever he was doing drove me insane with lust. I thrummed against him, my hips rocking. With each lick, my neck stung but left me utterly gasping. And a deep pulse speared through me, my body strung so tight, but somehow Ares drove me farther and farther.

Yet, my wolf rumbled in my chest, and my mind was torn in two... between pushing Ares away and asking for more. Though it was hard to tell when my mind blurred.

He unleashed a deep, guttural sound in my ear.

Then my world detonated, and I tilted my head back, the desperate cry of my orgasm piercing the night. He never ceased devouring my neck, even when I shoved my hands against him. But the sensation of arousal still fogged my head.

"My little dove, you are delicious," I heard him whisper.

His attentiveness never eased, while the combination of my orgasm, his tight hold, and the warning bells going off in the back of my head that something was wrong was becoming too much.

Darkness feathered at the corners of my eyes, and I blinked, falling into its depth.

———

I woke with a gasp on my lips and a burning heat between my thighs. I stared at the white ceiling, then glanced over to Daxon, who was dead to the world in his bed next to me. His deep breathing told me my abrupt waking up didn't even register with him.

My heart was pitter-pattering faster in my chest as I vaguely remembered what happened last night.

But I had no clue how in the world I ended up back in bed with Daxon.

Snippets of last night floated to the surface of my mind.

Sleepwalking into the woods.

The monster that nearly attacked me.

Ares saved me, tried to kiss me... then after that, things got a bit blurry.

Looking over at Daxon, I knew if he found out about the kiss, he'd go bat-shit crazy and murder Ares. Even I wanted to pepper Ares with questions about what actually happened. Why I couldn't clearly remember everything.

Pushing my legs out of bed, I got to my feet, and my hand instinctively went to clasp the side of my neck. Ares had bitten me.

Or was that just a dream?

My fingers traced the smooth skin on my neck that held no sign of a bite.

I wrinkled my nose with confusion.

Making my way into the bathroom, I glanced in the mirror at my reflection with wild hair and dark shadows under my eyes, like I hadn't slept for a week. Then I tilted my head to the side to better view my neck

Not a blemish on my skin.

Had I really dreamed the whole thing? *Please, I didn't want to end up going crazy.*

I washed my face with cold water, starting to feel slightly batty, like I might be losing my mind.

Toweling my face dry, I glanced down to my feet. They were filthy, covered in dirt and mud. I *had* been in the woods... that part was true.

And just then, a slight tingle grazed the side of my neck, the same buzz coursing through me as I'd felt when his teeth had slid into my skin.

Staring back at my unmarked neck, I gripped the edges of the sink as a shiver ran over me. I couldn't stop thinking of him, and why couldn't I remember much?

Had it all happened in my sleepwalking trance?

10

RUNE

My insides were a mess as I walked down the street aimlessly, wishing I could shift and get away from it all.

"Rune," Mr. Jones called after me. I closed my eyes and let out a sigh, wondering if I could just pretend that I didn't hear him.

"Rune, please," he called again, sounding distraught at the notion that I was ignoring him.

I rolled my shoulders back and turned around, keeping a blank look on my face as he hurried to catch up to me.

"What do you want?" I asked coldly, not really interested in hearing excuses from one more person in my life who had disappointed me.

"I just wanted to apologize....for everything. When Miyu came to me and asked me to talk, she seemed so distraught. And she was so convinced you'd been having an affair with her mate. I—I'm very sensitive about that subject, and I made a mistake."

I studied him for a long moment, wondering what in

his past he was referencing. He was a mystery dressed up in a sharp suit.

"That's the second time that I've been drugged by you," I snapped, not feeling particularly forgiving.

"The first time I was just trying to help you relax!" he replied stiffly, obviously affronted.

My fists clenched as I tried to keep control of myself. "I haven't had very many times that I've been in control of my life, and now that I've finally escaped from that, I don't appreciate losing control once again because of my so-called friends!"

Mr. Jones's shoulders slumped, and his whole body tremored as he pulled on his suit despondently.

"My mate cheated on me...with my best friend. They carried the affair on for years apparently, and one day I came home early...and caught them. It was long ago, but I obviously haven't been able to let it go," he said in a choked-up voice.

The anger I'd been holding onto snapped at that admission. "Oh, Mr. Jones," I whispered, tears welling up in my eyes as I watched him try and hold himself together.

"Come into the cafe and have a treat with me. I swear on my life there won't be any tricks. I have everything you like."

"Okay," I said softly, resisting the urge to hug the distraught man. I understood being a slave to the past. I was a mess ninety-nine percent of the time thanks to everything Alistair had done to me. Add in the fact that I watched the woman I thought was my mother be killed, along with the fact that I'd found out she wasn't my mother at the same time...and I didn't know if it was possible for me to ever truly trust someone.

I followed him into the cafe, thinking about the fact

that with everything that had been going on, I hadn't even had a chance to think about my mother's death and the truth she had given me.

I didn't even know how to start trying to find out who my real parents were.

There was a part of me that was afraid to find out their identity, though. Would they disappoint me just like everyone else in my life had?

My thoughts were disrupted when I walked into the cafe and the usual incredible scents passed over me. You would think they wouldn't smell good to me now after what had happened, but sugar plus coffee was a hard thing to beat.

"Sit right here and I'll grab some things," Mr. Jones said quickly, gesturing to an empty table near the dessert display. He hustled behind the counter like he was afraid I was going to change my mind at any minute.

There were a few other townspeople in the cafe, seated at other tables and shooting me their usual distrustful looks.

Someday I would get used to that.

Mr. Jones was back then, setting down five plates heaped high with desserts that looked and smelled incredible.

"I've got my blueberry streusel coffee cake, my vanilla loaf cake, my cinnamon chocolate muffin, and my caramel funfetti sprinkle bread that I just came up with the other day. Oh, and there's a sugar cookie latte with sugar cookie cold foam and extra sprinkles to wash it all down," he explained, gesturing to it all with a flourish.

"Are you trying to say sorry or give me diabetes?" I teased, and he flushed and opened his mouth to say something right as a large crowd of people burst through the doors, talking and laughing with each other.

He looked torn as his gaze danced from the new influx of customers to me. "Go on," I said with a smile. "We can talk later after I eat your apologies," I told him, taking a big bite of his new concoction as a symbol of my forgiveness.

Any other anger I'd been carrying flew out the door as the treat hit my tongue. Holy hell, I'd found my new favorite thing. The caramel funfetti sprinkle bread needed to be called "better than sex" because it was the most fantastic thing that I'd ever tasted.

I was busy moaning my way through the desserts when a throat cleared from beside me. I frowned at being inter- rupted during my tastebud orgasm until I looked up and saw that Ares was standing right by me.

"Is that seat saved?" he asked with a smirk, holding up his cup and a plate of the same bread that I'd just inhaled.

"Nope, go ahead," I told him, shifting in my seat nervously as he smoothly sat down and took a long sip of what looked like coffee. Was he going to bring up the other night? Did I want him to bring up the other night?

Definitely not.

"What's the verdict?" he asked suddenly.

"Hmm?" I asked, my face flushing like he could read my mind and discover what I'd just been thinking about.

"What's the best treat here?" He gestured to my plate filled with half-eaten sweets. "You seem to have a sampling of everything right there."

I flushed as I stared down at the table filled with plates. It was a funny sight.

"You picked the best one already," I told him, nodding at his plate which held the caramel "better than anything I'd ever tasted in my life" cake. "But I do warn you, if you hadn't planned on your life being completely changed today, I would not proceed."

He snorted at my corniness and took an exaggerated, huge bite of the cake. "What the fuck," he said, the words coming out garbled with his full mouth. He swallowed and quickly grabbed another forkful. "I thought you were joking!"

I giggled at the expression of pure bliss on his face as he proceeded to scarf down the treat in the next few seconds.

"Think we can convince him to make us like five of those to take home?" he asked, looking serious.

I snorted and glanced at Mr. Jones who was still working hard to fulfill orders. Maybe I would ask him for that as an apology present.

"Decided when you're moving on?" I asked more seriously, ignoring the fact that the idea was actually...sad.

"I've decided I'll be sticking around," he said casually, his gaze roving over my features like he was trying to memorize them.

I leaned forward, a pulse of excitement passing through me. "Oh, really?" I responded as casually as I could muster.

He smirked like he could see right through me.

"What made you decide that?"

"Do you really want to know the answer to that, Rune?" he asked, amused.

"Um—"

Just then, a little girl who'd been sitting with her mother at the next table threw herself onto the ground and began to sob hysterically. Her exhausted-looking mother was bouncing a baby up and down in her lap and begging the girl to get off the floor.

With a small pop, the toddler abruptly turned into a tiny tawny-colored wolf pup, and she began to pull on the tablecloth with a low growl. The mom jumped up to try and stop her, but the baby started to scream hysterically. The mother's cheeks flushed in embarrassment as she tried to soothe the baby and grab the mischievous pup.

"I've got her," Ares said with a grin that showed off a dimple on the left side of his cheek. How had I not noticed that before? He scooped the pup off the ground, holding her gently, and began to pet her softly, whispering soft coos to her that had my insides going haywire.

Seeing this huge, hot guy holding this tiny little wolf pup was dangerous to my panties.

Nope, Rune. We aren't going there.

The pup licked Ares' face and snuggled into him as she gazed up at him in adoration.

I found myself watching him with the same rapt attention that she was. Ares looked totally at ease holding her, and his already beyond attractive grin only widened when he caught me staring at him. Was there drool coming out of my mouth? I picked up a napkin and dabbed at my mouth... just in case.

"She's good. Go ahead and feed your baby," he cajoled the frazzled-looking woman who immediately shot him a grateful grin and dug through her bag, grabbing a bottle for her still crying baby.

"You look pretty comfortable there," I teased as he settled back into the chair across from me, gently petting the blissful-looking pup who appeared to be seconds away from falling asleep.

"There were ten other kids in one of my foster homes, all younger than me. Let's just say I got a lot of experience with little kids," he explained softly as the pup burrowed even closer into his chest.

"Foster home?" I asked hesitantly, not wanting to prod

but definitely interested in another glimpse into this stranger's past.

"Yeah. My parents were found guilty of betraying the royal family and were beheaded as traitors when I was six," he said matter-of-factly even as my jaw dropped at the information he was sharing.

"The royal family? Traitors?" I asked, not sure what to ask first.

He cocked his head, a curious look in his eyes as he studied me. "You've never heard of the Atlandia royal family?"

I shook my head, frowning as I leaned in closer, wondering how that was possible.

"For around a thousand years, there was a ruling family in power that was basically over all of the packs in Europe. There was a time they were the ruling family over most of the world's shifter packs even before that, but over the centuries, their power waned," he began.

"How have I never heard of this?" I asked, confused.

"Around twenty years ago, the whole family was wiped out. The king, the queen, the prince...even the extended family. They weren't rulers over the American packs, so it wouldn't have been discussed that much when you were a child. It was all kept hush-hush because of the fear it brought to the old shifter packs in Europe. No one knows how it happened."

"And there were no survivors?" I asked, shivering at the tale.

His eyes glimmered. "They never recovered one of the bodies. The princess. But most assume she was taken out of the castle walls to be disposed of."

I frowned, thinking about the poor little girl. "You said your parents were accused of betraying the royal family? So you're from Europe?" I asked. Everything he was saying sounded so fantastical, it was hard to imagine.

He nodded. "Five years before the royal family was massacred, my parents were accused of working with one of the noble families to plan an uprising."

"Were they actually doing that?"

He shrugged his shoulders, and the now sleeping pup whined at his movement. He softly trailed his finger from the top of her head, down her snout, and she immediately quieted.

"I'm going to call you the pup whisperer," I murmured, and he scoffed quietly.

"I don't really have any memories of my parents. My last name was changed and I was sent to the States to get away from the taint of my parent's actions. Thus the series of foster homes," he explained calmly, not seeming the least bit upset about the story he was telling. "I remember my parents. I remember them being gone and staying with strangers. I only found out the real details of what happened, though, when I got my file after I aged out of the foster system."

"I'm so sorry for your loss," I told him, my voice catching as I thought about my own mother...or fake mother dying.

Ares' gaze was locked with mine, and he swallowed before he tipped his head, emotions brimming In his eyes that I couldn't quite read.

"I lost my mother recently," I told him, not bothering to go into the fact that she hadn't been my real mother. "I think no matter how old you are, it hurts."

"Yes. It does," he responded in a gruff voice.

At that moment, the mother appeared next to us, her baby wrapped up in a carrier against her chest. "Thank you so much," she said softly, reaching out for her adorable sleeping tot nestled in Ares' arms.

"Anytime," he said with a wink, making the woman's cheeks flush...this time not from embarrassment.

I snorted softly, and he gave me a wink as well. He stood up and placed the toddler in the stroller that the woman was pushing in front of her, and miraculously, she stayed asleep. We both waved goodbye to her as she pushed the stroller towards the exit.

"You have another admirer," I commented.

"Would that be you, Rune? Because that's the only person I'm interested in for that role," he said seriously, watching me closely.

I squirmed in my chair, not knowing what to say. "Ares, I'm with Daxon...and well, Wilder and I are complicated." I swallowed, pain flickering through me once again just thinking about Wilder. "But I love them both."

Ares' midnight blue gaze continued to be intense as he stood up and rounded the table. He leaned over me until his lips were brushing against my ear. "I don't see a problem with that statement. Obviously, you're not an either/or kind of girl." Goosebumps spread all over my skin as his lips moved to my cheek, and then he was striding out of the cafe without a look back, leaving me a hot, frantic mess behind him.

What the fuck was that?

Wilder

I leaned against the brick wall, my gaze locked on Rune and Ares inside the cafe. She threw her head back and laughed, and my wolf growled in frustration.

"He's getting a little too close for comfort with her,

don't you think?" came Daxon's voice, and I flinched at him catching me watching her.

"Rune can do what she wants," I said stubbornly, still unable to take my eyes away from the scene.

"Cut the bullshit, Wilder. Man up," Daxon snapped.

My gaze cut to him, a warning growl low in my throat. Suddenly, dizziness overtook me, and I groaned as I closed my eyes and leaned back against the wall, trying to stay upright. I opened my eyes and stared around me, my gaze flicking to Rune. Why was I here watching her? Daria would be back in the next few days. I loved her.

Did I love her? Pain crashed in my head as I struggled to get my thoughts together.

"Wilder? Are you alright?" Daxon asked, concerned.

"Just a headache," I muttered, rubbing my temple desperately.

"Have you been getting those a lot?" Daxon asked casually, and I flicked him an annoyed glare.

"A fair amount," I admitted. "It's been a stressful time, I guess. With the fallout from Rune. And then getting with Daria. It's all been...a lot."

Why was I admitting this to Daxon of all people again?

"Yes," he said slowly, as if he was thinking hard. "Quite stressful. It was all quite sudden. I mean, one second you're hot and heavy with Rune, trying to make her your mate... and then poof, you're with Daria declaring your love. Kind of fickle, don't you think?"

Did I try to make Rune my mate? What the fuck?

"What?" I blurted out, my gaze darting back to where Ares was now standing by Rune, whispering in her ear.

Daxon growled next to me, and I saw his claws extend. "Which part did you not understand, asshole? I'm struggling to understand how one minute you were swearing your undying love to Rune, the most perfect woman on earth. And the next, you're doing the same thing with the fae bitch."

The pain in my head increased until it felt like my brain was in danger of bursting. Every time I tried to think about the end with Rune, it was like walking through fog.

My breaths began to come out in gasps as my chest tightened and my skin pebbled with sweat. The edges of my vision began to darken, and I slid down the wall.

"Whoa there. What's going on?" Daxon asked quickly.

"I—I don't know what's happening," I choked out as my hands began to shake.

"You're having a panic attack. Just try and take deep breaths," he commanded. I began to take exaggerated, long breaths, but Rune and Daria's faces kept flashing through my mind, and I couldn't get ahold of myself. What was wrong with me?

Abruptly, Daxon punched me, and I fell over in shock, the side of my cheek throbbing from the force of the hit.

"What the fuck?" I growled as I turned on him.

The bastard looked very satisfied as he stared down at me. "What was that for?"

"Oh, I owe you much more than that for breaking Rune's heart, but consider that a little gift. You're not freaking out anymore, right?"

I swallowed as I realized that all my symptoms had receded. Only the pain in my head was still there, pulsing away in my brain.

"Thanks," I said slowly. "I think."

Daxon crouched down next to me. "The only reason I'm even doing anything for your worthless ass is because she still cries for you every night. Remember that when this is all said and done."

"When what is said and done?" I asked, but Daxon was already striding away.

And of course, my gaze immediately drifted back to where Rune was sitting with a cute, confused look on her face.

Fuck.

11

RUNE

I stared out the open window like I'd found myself
doing every night lately. I didn't know if it was an
effort to be close to the Moon Goddess, or if it was
because part of me was wondering if Wilder was looking up
at the same moon as I was. I guess it could have been both.

Movement down below caught my eye...and there
he was.

Wilder stood in the shadows of the inn, watching me.
We locked eyes and he moved to leave.

"Wait," I called out. "Please, just stay there for one
minute. I'll be right down," I called to him before I rushed
from the window and grabbed my shoes. After slipping
them on, I dashed out of my room and down the stairs, a
steady chant in my head, praying that he hadn't gone away.

If I could just see him...just talk to him. I felt like a drug-
gie, desperate for another fix. Even if Wilder hated my guts,
my heart didn't care. I just needed to see him. Just for a
moment.

I rushed out into the chilly air and came to a surprised
halt when I saw that Wilder was still there, standing in the

shadows. I devoured the perfect angles of his face, filing away mental pictures of him to hold onto later when he inevitably disappeared once again.

I took a step towards him and he quickly stepped back, determined to keep his distance from me. My shoulders sagged. The weight of my sadness felt like an oppressive burden shackled to my back. "Why are you here, Wilder?" I asked sadly, wondering how my heart could hurt this badly and still be beating.

"I—I can't stop myself," he finally admitted in a soft, gruff voice. "My wolf has to be near you. He's going crazy without you."

My eyes widened at his admission, but then I realized it didn't mean anything because the other side of him...wanted her.

"And what about you?" I asked, the question slipping out even though I regretted it the second it was gone from my lips.

There was a long, heavy silence. "I feel like I have to be near you too. You're like a wound that just won't heal, an empty space that won't fill no matter what I do. Why can't I let you go?" His words come out as just a whisper, but I tremble under their power.

"I still love you," I tell him honestly, even if I'm coming to hate that love at the same time.

He was there in front of me then, pushing me against the wall and melding my body against his. His lips were on me, his tongue parting mine as he devoured me like never before. His fingers grabbed onto my hair, moving my head this way and that so we were always at the perfect angle for this kiss. This fucking perfect kiss that I was worried would become just another memory meant to taunt and torture me as the days went by and he still wasn't mine.

"I'm so tired of fighting this feeling. I'm tired of keeping myself away from you," he groaned against my lips, and I shivered despite the fact that my body felt like it had caught fire.

"Come upstairs with me," I whispered desperately. Just one night. I had to have it. If he disappeared then, maybe I could let him go for good.

But I needed this right now or I felt like I was going to die.

What Daxon and Wilder didn't understand was that it was never about owning half my heart. They each owned all of it somehow. I loved them both so much that I knew there was nothing half-hearted about the feeling. It was magical, all-encompassing.

And before lately, I'd thought maybe it could be forever.

But I wouldn't think about that now. I would just think about tonight, this moment. Even if it turned out to be the last time.

Maybe it made me pathetic, but I loved both of them so much I could probably forgive them for anything when it came down to it.

His face moved away from mine, and he just stared at me, looking torn. I'm sure desperation was written all over my face. But I didn't care.

And then I was in his arms and he was practically running into the inn and up the stairs, taking a break halfway up to give me the full weight of his mouth once more as our tongues tangled frantically together.

Our lips never stopped moving against each other as he got us up the flight of the stairs and to my room, and didn't my wolf just love the fact that he knew the exact room we were staying in.

"What are you doing to me, Rune?" he asked desperately once we got inside and his hands were sliding all over the skin that was showing outside of my flimsy nightgown. His skin was somehow burning up despite the fact he'd been outside in the cold, and I moaned as his lips traced down my neck until he was focused on the racing pulse in my neck. He trembled as he touched me, and it somehow calmed me down, knowing that he was feeling this torrent of emotion just like I was.

My nightgown disappeared as his hands continued to move all over me, followed by the soft sigh of his lips.

He scooped me up and placed me on my bed almost reverently, awe in his gaze as he stared at my naked form encased by the bright moonlight shining in from the window. His eyes raked over every inch of me and his chest rose and fell rapidly as he took it all in. He fell to his knees suddenly, and his mouth began to feast on me, parting my folds and devouring every inch until I was a quaking, writhing mess. He moaned as he licked, and sucked, and bit until I was a second away from bursting into a million pieces.

He pushed away from me with a gasp, his lips shiny from my cum. "I have to be inside of you," he growled before tearing at his shirt, the buttons flicking all over the room. He yanked his pants off with the same inpatient, jerky movements, and then he was standing there completely naked. I devoured his perfect form, wondering how he and Daxon were such gods above men.

For a second, Ares' face flickered in my mind, but I quickly torched that image and sent it up in a million fiery mental flames. That was a path I wasn't even taking a step down.

Wilder took a step towards me, and just as I thought I

was ready for him, Daria's face assaulted my mind this time.

"Wait," I said, not believing that I was doing this right now.

"What is it, baby?" he said as he slowly stroked himself while his eyes feasted on my naked skin. I shifted nervously on the bed, feeling the urge to cover up. I definitely didn't want to know the answer to this question, but I felt like I had to ask. I couldn't not.

"Have you slept with her?" I whispered, unable to look him in the face as the words slipped out. I shouldn't even be bringing her up right now, but I couldn't help it. She was this invisible specter with us in the room right now.

He immediately stopped stroking himself and flinched as if I'd shot him.

"Rune," he began, and I swore my heart split in half as I prepared for the worst. "I—I'm a piece of shit even talking about this right now, but no, I haven't even been able to get close. I—all I can think about is you."

I swore my heart stitched back together at that moment, and a flicker of hope dashed through my veins.

Before he could say anything, I reached up and yanked him towards me. I had no control as my hands roamed over him, savoring the feel of his skin against mine, something I wasn't sure I'd ever experience again. His lips moved over my chest, his tongue and mouth making me arch into him as he swirled his tongue around my nipples. My hands tangled in his hair, and I stifled a moan. It felt so fucking good. He spread my legs wide as his fingers traveled lightly across my stomach towards my heat. I gasped again as he brushed gently through my folds, a low groan coming out of him as he realized how wet I was.

"Tell me this is okay," he growled as if in pain, and I

nodded desperately as he slid into me with one swift move. Our breaths came out in ragged gasps of relief as if we'd been missing a part of ourselves this whole time and only now were we complete.

"I just need to be still for a moment," he groaned as his eyes closed and his face scrunched up. "I'm so close already."

I giggled, and he licked up the side of my cheek playfully. "You think it's funny how crazy you make me?"

I could feel my smile beaming back at him; the happiness inside of me was a living, breathing thing.

"I love you," I told him. His cheek pulsed, and he looked pained as I wrapped my legs around his hips, pushing him even further inside of me.

"I can't remember how it used to be between us, Rune. It all feels like a blur. But I know that this feeling is unlike anything I've ever experienced. I—don't understand how I can love you...and hate you all at the same time."

I frowned, thinking that was an odd way to phrase it. *How it used to be*...like it had been years instead of weeks since we'd been together every day.

"I hate you too," I whispered, thinking it was somehow true. I loved him with everything in me, but I hated him for making me hurt like this too. I didn't know what he was feeling, but when I thought back to the conversation right before he'd walked away, I was sure he was feeling a bit of hate that day as well.

A strong conviction embedded itself into my bloodstream at that moment. I knew something wasn't right. Maybe it should have been obvious right away but I'd been trapped in a veil of self-pity that made it hard to see clearly. I knew without a shadow of a doubt that Wilder had loved me even when he walked away. There was no way that he'd suddenly "forget" in such a short time everything we'd meant to each other. Daria had done something. Or someone had done something.

But Wilder was mine. There was no other endgame. I'd find a way to make everything okay. And I'd only let him go if I was convinced it was what *he* really wanted, not someone else out there in the world.

He brushed his lips against mine, clearly feeling the weight of the moment just as deeply as I was. I arched against him, forcing him to move, the feeling of him deep inside me making me ache for more.

"Rune," his voice growled as he finally began to move with me. "Fuck. You feel perfect."

"Please," I whispered desperately against his neck. Without another word, his hips began to move powerfully in and out of me again and again. He wrapped both arms around me, pulling me so close that I could hear the beat of his heart tumbling around in his chest.

I couldn't restrain the moan that ripped from my throat as our bodies joined together. A fire flickered up inside me, burning brighter and brighter as we moved. His hands, his lips pushed me quickly to the edge. His breath was hot against my neck as my head fell back, giving in to pure sensation. I felt the tightness in my stomach explode once again, my ragged breathing turning into a long-broken moan as I spiraled over the edge.

I saw his eyes widen as I cried out with the force of my release. He continued to move hungrily as he chased his own ending. His head fell back as he came, our breaths and moans a sexual symphony that I could have listened to forever.

We collapsed on the bed, both of us gasping for breath.

He spoke softly moments later.

"How did I lose this?" he breathed against my skin, and my arms clenched him even tighter against me. I didn't have an answer. I only knew that even if we were lost right now, I wouldn't let us be lost forever.

I'd find a way to bring him back to me.

My heart was racing, anticipating the end before he even left as his fingers softly stroked down my bare skin that was pebbled under the cool air.

I tried my best not to fall asleep. I wanted the moment to last forever.

But somehow I did.

And when I woke up, he was gone, no trace of him left behind except for the ache between my legs and the love bites on my neck.

As if it had been nothing but a dream.

12

RUNE

I drew in a deep breath that failed miserably to calm my pounding heart. Walking into Mr. Jones' cafe shot my adrenaline up...it shouldn't have, since he had apologized about drugging me.

But I was meeting Miyu, and the last time I'd caught up with her at the cafe...it didn't exactly go well.

Earlier in the day, she had popped into the diner during my morning shift and asked me to meet up with her afterward.

She was still my friend, and I wanted to patch things up between us... somehow. Even if I was still furious at her for what she did to me.

Locals filled the cafe, and there were no spare tables. Mr. Jones tipped his hat at my entrance, but he was so run off his feet, making coffees and serving baked goods, he wasn't being his usual jovial host. The aroma of coffee filled the room, as did the buzz of chatter.

I was scanning the room when Mr. Jones rushed past me with two coffees in hand, saying, "She's in the back booth waiting for you." Then he was gone.

"Thanks," I said, not that he could hear my response, and I started forward past the busy tables and into the far corner. A dangling lamp hung over the booth that had no windows. The spot was tucked away and would make the perfect hideaway for settling in to read a book on a cold day.

I joined Miyu and took a seat across from her in the booth.

"Hey," she said, her voice mildly shaken, eyes red like she'd been crying. But she attempted to put a smile on her face, which gave me hope that this might be a chance to make up.

"How have you been?" I asked, wanting to reach out and take her hand in mine, wishing we could put everything behind us so I could hug her and tell her things would eventually be all right. That I was there for her.

But she licked her lips before taking a long drink from her glass of water, keeping her distance.

"I have something to show you," she answered instead, and twisted to her side where she rummaged through her large handbag. I noticed her messy hair hadn't been combed, and the black and white striped tee she wore was inside out. My insides clenched at seeing her falling apart.

I should have made more of an effort to go visit her. Her drugging me came from a place of desperation and heart-wrenching grief. I hated how horrible I felt for her.

"What is it?" I asked softly.

She turned back around and placed an oversized white coffee mug on the table with the words *Don't Mess With The Chefasaurus* across the front. It still had dried coffee stains on the lip and a drip on the outside.

"This was Rae's cup. He used it every day and even took it to work sometimes. He loved this hideous thing. It didn't match anything in our kitchen, but he refused to let it go. It was a gift from his grandmother, you see."

I nodded, not quite following where we were going with the conversation, but I also didn't want to not appear invested or caring.

"And I won't accept that Rae was ever a monster, so I turned the house upside down, going through everything to understand what I missed about him. And how he could actually kill anyone." She was talking so fast, blinking, and I suspected she hardly slept last night.

"Okay, and what did you find?" I stared at the cup, still completely befuddled.

"Smell it," she said and pushed the mug across the table toward me.

My shoulders reared back, and I was really trying here, but now I worried that Miyu had lost her mind.

"Miyu, are you okay? I know we haven't been seeing eye to eye lately, but I'm always here—"

"Just smell the damn cup," she snapped. "I'm not going crazy, and if you are my friend, then you'll hear me out and give me the benefit of doubt."

"Okay," I replied and lifted it to my nose. At first, just the stale stench of coffee filled my nostrils. And it wasn't pleasant. I crinkled my nose at it, but there were other faint smells too. The ceramic of the cup and, barely noticeable, an acrid smell that gave a slight sting in my nostrils.

"You smell it, don't you?" she asked, leaning forward on her folded arms against the table.

"What is it?" I kept sniffing it, unable to identify the scent.

"Poison," she whispered.

My gaze met hers. "Are you serious?"

She was smiling wide, her eyes crazy as if she'd just

discovered the long-lost burial chamber of an Egyptian God. "My theory is that someone was poisoning Rae and making him go all psycho."

I frowned and set the cup down. "Who would do that and why?"

She shrugged and collected the mug hastily from in front of me, then stuffed it back into her bag. "I took the cup to several people in town, including the doctor, and they all confirmed the smell was some kind of poison. Without testing it, they wouldn't know specifically which one. But think about it. For all the years I've known Rae, why would he only start killing more recently? If he is the cold-blooded killer Daxon thinks him to be, wouldn't he have left more bodies behind long before now? His behavior just wasn't adding up. He'd become more distant recently, and whoever was poisoning him must have done it more frequently because he had never acted that way before. All distant and withdrawn."

How could I deny it when she made sense? And I definitely smelled something weird in that cup that didn't belong there.

"You know, this might explain a peculiarity I'd picked up at each of the murders," I said. "There was never a wolf scent left behind on the victim. So, what if that poison concealed his scent?" My mind was going into overdrive now with all kinds of theories, when I asked, "Did you check the coffee jar?"

Miyu nodded. "Yep. There was no scent on it at all. It's like someone broke into our home just to place poison into his cup. Who the fuck would go to that length?" Her expression tightened, while her eyes teared up. "What had we done to anyone for them to hurt my Rae this way?"

That time, the tears fell, and I quickly moved across to

sit next to her, taking her into my arms as she cried against my shoulder. Her body shook, and my eyes pricked at her agony. Pain flared in the middle of my chest from the grief.

When she finally broke away and opened her tear-drenched eyes, she wiped her cheeks and gave me a lopsided grin. "I promised myself I wouldn't cry today. Well, I broke that rule."

"There's no limit on grieving. Take as long as you need. Cry until you drown the town. Do what you need," I said, rubbing her arm.

"I suspect someone was using Rae as a puppet for a distraction or to carry out their work. I kept going over it in my mind, and I don't think it's the werewolf hunters, since they would just swoop in and kill. This is something more sinister, and I will find out who did this to us."

"I'm so sorry, Miyu."

"Just so we're clear, what Daxon did wasn't right. And I don't know if I can forgive him right now...or ever."

I licked my lips and collected her trembling hand in mine. "I understand that. He and I are working through a few things right now too." My heart sped up just thinking of how much he meant to me, but how much more difficult things had become.

Her head was down, eyes focused on Rae's cup half sticking out of her bag.

"I'll do everything to help you find out who did this."

Her head shot up, a loose tear threading down her cheek, which she swiped away. "Then you believe me that someone made Rae kill those people by poisoning him and making him go crazy?"

As insane as it sounded, I believed her, and with it came a stinging ache in my heart to know that someone had purposefully done this to Rae. I wanted to think that Daxon might regret taking his life, but I had been there when Rae lost control, and he was terrifying. In Daxon's shoes, I would have done the same thing to stop any more deaths.

"I do," I answered. "In the time I'd known him, Rae had been so kind to me, making jokes in the kitchen, and being so kind to everyone at the diner. Rae was genuine. And I believe that someone must have poisoned him to make him lose control."

She threw herself into my arms and hugged me tightly. "Thank you. I just needed to hear that so I stopped feeling like I was going crazy."

"We'll work this out together," I said, patting her back.

"Ladies, I've brought you a complimentary plate of treats. Figured you could both use something sweet." Mr. Jones' voice drew us apart, and we both looked up at the man placing a large plate with an assortment of his pastries and cake slices in front of us.

"Wow, that's a lot," I said, shifting to face the table as Miyu sniffled and pushed her hair out of her face. "But I'm already eyeing the brownie."

"I feel horrible that you both had a falling out," Mr. Jones said, his mouth downturned. "And if the glue to put you both back together is baked goods, then I'll supply you with them until you can no longer fit into your dresses."

I burst out laughing. "A nice gesture, but you don't need to worry. We are slowly making up, right, Miyu?"

She nodded. "Definitely."

"Oh," he said. "Well then, I guess you won't be needing this plate." He grinned and playfully went to retrieve his goodies.

I quickly grabbed it and brought it back toward us. "These are staying," I said possessively, narrowing my eyes at him before laughing.

"I'm glad." He wiped his hands down his small, black apron. "I'll leave you with an old Irish proverb that has guided me well in life. A good friend is like a four-leaf clover. They're hard to find and lucky to have. Enjoy your treats, ladies."

"He may be onto something," Miyu added before pawing at the treats and taking a slice of chocolate cake covered in ganache.

Somehow, between us, we managed to finish the whole plate. My stomach was bloated, but I had no regrets. Sometimes, drowning in food was completely acceptable.

I leaned back in the booth and glanced over to Miyu who pushed the last morsel of cake into her mouth.

"So, how are we going to find out who poisoned Rae?" I asked.

"I have a plan," Miyu said, then wiped her mouth. "I have to guess that the person responsible lives in town. How else would they have known Rae's everyday routine and when to sneak into our home, right?"

"But whoever did it won't be watching your home anymore," I answered.

"I know, but psychopaths love to watch the outcome of the chaos they unleashed. So, it would be someone who will be paying extra attention to me. Someone I least suspect."

"Yep. But hang on," I said. "What's the plan then? Take note of everyone who looks at you, comes near you? That's going to be hard in town when everyone goes about their own day."

"I've thought of that, but in a few days, there's a town celebration being held, and everyone will be in one place. It's the perfect spot to observe anyone who watches me too carefully."

"Town celebration? What's that?" I ran my fingers over the crumbs on the table and dusted them off into the plate.

"Didn't Daxon tell you? He and Wilder had organized a gathering to help bring some calm over the packs after all the bad things that have happened in town."

I might have lost my breath as I attempted to process her words. "Wait, did you say they are working together? Are you sure you got that right?" My mind flew to how strange Wilder had been lately, how distant he was, and yet he'd turned up at my window the other night. His words and actions confused me, but I knew deep in my soul, I still loved him. Then there was Daxon, who didn't give a shit about Wilder, so what was I missing?

In a perfect world, Daxon and Wilder would get along and gladly share me. Rae would still be alive, and there would be no monsters stalking the woods.

"You look shocked," Miyu murmured.

"Considering everything that's happened lately, this is news to me." Not to mention, Daxon never said anything to me about the party. I was slightly offended that he'd forgotten me in his grand plan. Or did he have something else orchestrated for me? That thought slightly scared me. Of course, my thoughts flew to my night with Wilder. Maybe Daxon had somehow found out and was now planning some kind of retaliation.

While part of me couldn't deny that he'd try to get revenge in some way against Wilder, I also wanted to believe the party would be an honest attempt to bring union between the pack members and alleviate their worries after all the deaths.

"Well, it's happening," Miyu said, distracting me from my thoughts. "I heard directly from Daxon that he and Wilder are coordinating a huge party soon for all of us"

"Then it should make for an interesting night," I said, trying to make light of the moment and not let myself get caught up in my woes.

Miyu fell quiet, and she was staring at Rae's mug in her bag, looking broken. A tear slid down her cheek she never wiped away. My chest clenched, seeing how unstable she was, how grief was swallowing her whole.

I started to wonder if her chasing down the person responsible for Rae's death was such a good idea. She was fragile in her state. And when she looked up at me, her lips tugged into a painful smile like that was the only way to stop more tears from falling.

My eyes pricked for her, and I hurt seeing her falling apart before my eyes.

"Hey, I have an idea," I suggested. "How about I speak with Daxon about the poison in Rae's mug, and we let him search for the person responsible? He'll do a better job than us anyway, and then you and I can just enjoy the party together?"

She blinked at me, and I watched the struggle behind her eyes.

I held onto her hand. "Daxon has experience in hunting down monsters. What do you say? I can let him know?"

Chewing on her lower lip, she glanced back to her bag and then at me. She gave me a small nod. "I'd like that." Her brittle response filled me with relief, with the hope that I could spend more time helping her with the trauma. "Thank you," she whispered.

"No problem. But first, how about we head back to your place, and I can make sure you're not wearing your shirt inside out." I smiled gently, teasing her to see if I could make her laugh a bit.

She glanced down at herself, poking at the seam

running down the outside of her sleeve, and gave out a small eek.

"I was in a rush this morning," she frowned. "I feel like I'm living in a bubble and can't think straight."

Reaching over, I took her hand in mine. "Don't worry about it. I accidentally wear my clothes inside out when I'm actually paying attention to what I'm wearing." I gave her a wonky grin.

"I'm just in a bad place mentally." She sighed. "I think I'm still super dysfunctional right now. So, thank you, Rune, for not abandoning me. And I'm sorry for using a truth serum on you. I never should have done that."

"I'm always here for you." I threw an arm around her shoulders, and I hugged her, needing her to know she wasn't alone. Then we both shuffled out of the booth.

"Oh, I almost forgot," she said, red rimming her eyes, her chin trembling. "I've arranged for a small funeral for Rae. Will you attend with me?" With her voice shaking, I held her closer.

"Of course." She wiped her cheeks, and I took her arm, walking us out of the cafe before we both bawled our eyes out even more.

Out on the sidewalk, she leaned against me, sniffling. "The way I miss Rae seems to come in waves. Some days I just weep, others I do everything to keep myself busy. And today, I'm drowning."

At her words, my chest tightened and tears gathered in my eyes, and anger rose within me. Whoever had targeted Rae not only ruined his life but everyone else's who knew him.

13

DAXON

I'd never liked Wilder, and I'd never made an effort to hide how I truly felt about him either. After the shit that went down between us and Arcadia, I'd struggled to be in the same room with him without feeling the urge to smash my fist into his face.

And wasn't it just the case that I found myself entangled with him again over another girl. Fate had a fucking sick sense of humor.

There was a huge difference in this one, though. Rune was nothing like Arcadia. She was trying to survive in this fucked up world, and she loved passionately with every fiber of her being.

Arcadia had been a bitch who used everyone. And it took me way too long to realize the truth.

Rune was pure of heart, and it was one of the reasons I'd given my heart and soul to her, why I'd burn down the whole world if it saved her.

And that meant going against my better judgment when it came to Wilder. As much as it fucking killed me, I was going to find out what the hell had screwed him up and made him leave Rune. Because if Wilder was even a fraction in love with her as I was, he'd have his ass with her. Not with the bitch fae queen.

Because of that, I found myself hidden in an alley, staring out as the duo strolled down the sidewalk, hand in hand. Something was utterly wrong with this picture. I remembered how much Wilder had hated Daria when we'd visited her to get help with Rune's heat, and for him to do a complete flip of his feelings still baffled my mind. Or did I have this all wrong? Was Wilder so fucking pissed that he had to share Rune, he'd rather leave her?

I shook my head... I doubted that. Wilder was a lot of things, but he wasn't an idiot. And only an idiot would lose a sweetheart like my girl.

Keeping my gaze on Wilder and Daria, I kept reminding myself I was doing this for Rune. At the end of the day, if my attempt to get him to open his eyes failed, then fuck him. I'd give Rune the world, anything she wanted to never think of him again.

I slipped out from the alleyway and tracked behind them from a distance.

Wilder walked rigidly, like he had something up his ass. I laughed under my breath, thinking it fit him. What did Rune see in him again?

Daria was draped over his arm, fawning over him. Talk about being insecure.

They headed into one shop after another.

"Afternoon, Daxon," someone said so abruptly from behind me that I snapped toward the man with a growl on my throat.

"Fuck off."

He backed away quickly, and I hastily swung back around. Wilder started to look back in my direction. *Shit.* I threw myself into the nearest store because I didn't need him knowing I was spying on him. Not until I knew what the fucking deal was between him and Daria.

I watched them from behind a rack of women's dresses through the window as they crossed the road and walked briskly towards a different store.

"Everything all right, Daxon?" a woman asked behind me, her voice slightly alarmed. I probably looked ridiculous darting around in between buildings like I was James Bond or something.

I straightened and offered Virginia a tight grin. "All good."

"Are you looking for a gift for your better half?" she quipped.

I shook my head, my eyes on Wilder, not having time for small talk. Without another word, I marched outside and rushed across the road, trailing after them.

Daria was giggling at something, then running her hands all over Wilder's arm and back... even his ass. I found it peculiar how hands-on she was with him... the bitch was fucking obsessed. Wilder barely responded to her touch, and any time he did touch her, it seemed forced. Yet he remained by her side.

That was strange, right? The longer I watched their interaction, the more it felt one-sided. And if that was the case, why the hell was that dick staying with her?

They paused to speak to some locals, Daria carrying on as though she belonged here and the pack members loved her. And Wilder went along with it, which had my heart pounding with fury.

I had known him for a long time... and in that time, I'd never seen him become such a damn pussy pushover.

For the next hour, I tracked after them, observing them,

trying to listen to their stilted conversation. Things just weren't adding up.

Daria fake laughed at someone's joke, cackling like a witch, her chest pressed into Wilder's side as she hugged him.

My eyes wanted to roll, but I was too busy trying not to hurl at the sight. This was a complete joke, and Wilder had found himself blindly following... he just didn't seem to realize it.

It didn't take a genius though to see the truth once you really paid attention to that situation. Wilder wasn't a pushover. He was a ruthless asshole and fought for everything, so this wasn't like him one bit. And on his arm was a fae queen... a dangerous woman who had power in her veins.

Everything inside of me was telling me she'd spelled him. There was no other way to explain the bullshit I was witnessing.

Heaving out a breath, I remained in my hiding spot around the corner of the bar, debating what I should do. I didn't exactly have the time to call in someone with magic to tell me if he had been cursed.

I'd have to handle it myself.

And there was only one way to deal with this love spell if it did exist... sever the connection between the pair. And I knew exactly how I'd do that. I'd been around various supernaturals enough to have picked up some knowledge on magic.

The longer I stared at Wilder's fake smile, the more I knew I had to save him. I was doing this for Rune, not him, but I wouldn't deny that my gut churned seeing him under Daria's control.

I grinned when my decision settled in my mind. It

would mean having to watch them until the time was right, but one way or another, I'd make Wilder a free man today.

Satisfied with my plan, I followed them, hopeful they'd finally leave the main part of town. There was simply no reason to assume Wilder wasn't under a spell, so this would work.

Or at least that's what I would tell myself.

The longer they dragged their feet, the more I groaned under my breath, but when they finally traipsed their way toward Wilder's new cabin, I grinned.

I moved quicker now, closing the distance and using the homes and trees as my cover. I was well versed in moving with silence.

They kept on chatting... Well, when I said *they*, I meant Daria while Wilder nodded.

When she fell silent suddenly, I froze and threw myself over a white picket fence, lying flat on the ground on my stomach. I sure as hell didn't need her casting a spell on me. Peering out from the gaps in the wooden fence, I watched her looking back down the street, and when she was satisfied that she was alone with Wilder, she curled her arm around his tighter.

They resumed their ascending stroll once more to the end of the street, making their way to the dark-timber cabin. The place stood on an elevated spot that overlooked the town.

Back up on my feet, I rushed after them, sticking closer to the trees crowding in the farther I rushed up the street.

When they reached their small front yard, and Wilder wandered to collect something from his lawn, I decided to make my move.

I lunged toward her, my hand collecting the weapon from my belt, holding it tight by my side. The wind played in my favor for a change, and silence enveloped me.

But my shadow gave me away. Never mind... too late for that now.

A swish of her skirt fabric and Daria spun around toward me. Huge eyes were what I saw first, then her mouth fell open, a wincing sound coming from her throat. Warm blood spilled over my hand from where I'd thrust the blade into her soft flesh, just under her ribcage.

"Time for the wicked witch to die," I growled.

She groaned, her hands clutching her wound, stumbling back. I yanked the knife out of her, needing her to bleed out.

"W-Wilder," she gurgled, blood seeping from the corners of her mouth. The way she called for Wilder almost sounded genuine, like she cared for him. Maybe she did... but that still made her dangerous.

Wilder turned on me like a beast, eyes on fire, teeth bared, and he threw a fist into my jaw so hard, stars danced in my eyes.

"Fuck!" I roared, staggering backward.

But when I caught myself before falling over, Wilder was no longer coming for me. He was on his knees, bellowing like a dying animal. A swirl of wind and dried leaves spun around him as though he sat in the middle of a vortex.

Magic... Goosebumps skittered over my skin as it grazed over me.

I threw my gaze to Daria and saw she was running away from us, into the woods, her hands clutching her wound, leaving a trail of blood behind in her wake. The wind seemed to almost carry her from us with how fast she moved.

Yep, she'd better run...

I then swung my attention to Wilder, who still moaned. The wind around him had settled, and his head lifted, agonizing green eyes meeting mine.

"What the fuck have you done?" he rasped.

I scrubbed a hand down my face. "I did you a favor. Trust me. It might not feel like it yet, but it will soon. You can thank me later."

His jawline clenched, working the muscles in his neck and straightening his back. But the moment he got to his feet, he stumbled like he'd been drinking for a week.

I jerked my arm forward and grabbed him so he didn't tumble over. I shouldn't care, but part of me felt pity for him. He'd had his share of bad luck. His cabin had burned down, then he'd been spelled to love someone he detested. That was fucked up. Not to mention the whole Arcadia thing.

"Steady," I said as he wrenched his arm from mine.

"Where's Daria?" He blinked rapidly as if he couldn't quite make sense of what just happened.

"She ran off with her tail between her legs, buddy. She put a love spell on you to become obsessed with her. She fucking tricked you so you'd leave Rune."

Confusion washed over his face, and I wasn't surprised. With love spells, lacerating the connection came in two parts. One, get rid of the fae as that weakened her connection over Wilder, and secondly, I needed to get the curse washed out of his system.

He kept rubbing his eyes. "Why the hell didn't you just tell me what the fuck was going on?"

I burst out laughing, unable to help myself. "Are you fucking joking? Are you even aware that she made you her puppet, and that she's been wearing you as her handbag?

There was no way the spell she put on you would let you see clearly. But it's done now, and you need to come with me so we can finish this."

His eyes scrunched shut, then opened again. "Why is my vision foggy? And my head is pounding."

"Because you're still infected by her poisonous spell." I snatched his elbow hard this time and dragged him into a walk down the street, making our way back to my place.

"H-how long have I been this way?" The pain in his voice angered me on his behalf. The next time I saw Daria, I would gut her from throat to groin for doing this to him... no one deserved the shit she pulled.

I held Wilder by my side, and we moved quickly, mostly to avoid onlookers starting to panic that their Alpha was hurt.

His black hair draped over his eyes, and he gave me a sideways glance, then looked around as we approached my cabin.

"Where are we going?"

"For a little drive," I answered just as we arrived at my car. Opening the passenger door, I nudged him to get in before shutting him inside. Racing around to the driver's seat, I was in and we were driving in a heartbeat.

Dust kicked in our rear from the tires skidding over the pebbled driveaway, and then we left the town behind.

"I don't understand how this happened," Wilder moaned.

"Well, Daria has wanted you as her sex toy since she first met you, although really, you should have never screwed around with the fae in the first place--"

"Fuck you, man. I don't need you reprimanding me," he growled, tugging at his seat belt, which seemed stuck.

I chuckled to myself...

"My guess is she got jealous of Rune and came into town to make you hers. You wouldn't have seen it coming, bruh. Fae don't tap you on the shoulder before cursing your ass."

"Don't be such a prick," he snarled and turned his attention to the woods we raced through. "I still feel drawn to her... it's weird, as the sensation is both familiar and foreign all at once. My wolf is thrashing inside me, pissed."

"He probably is after you left Rune and forced him to be with Daria," I said.

He sighed heavily, rubbing his face again.

I hit the gas so we traveled quicker, ascending the mountain, taking the sharp turns a bit too quickly. In the distance, the caps of the surrounding mountains rose sharply.

"Why are you speeding?" he snarled.

"It's fun," I answered.

Finally, I stopped atop the hill, and thankfully, Wilder hadn't said too much more. I just needed to get this done before Daria tried to call him and the spell got stronger. "Let's go," I ordered him.

With no hesitation, he got out and we moved through the woods.

"Do you know what you're doing?" he asked, climbing over a dead log.

"Yep. You're still infected by the fae, and if I don't get you cleansed, Daria will still own your ass. So, fewer questions and get a move on." The sun was lowering, and I'd wasted most of the day following him around town.

I heard the rush of water before we emerged out of the thick canopy and stepped onto the river's bank.

"You may not know this," I said. "But this water carries healing properties. "It's always been a sacred place and one of the reasons our families picked this location. The land was blessed, the waters purified."

When Wilder didn't respond, I glanced at him over my shoulder. Shadows darkened under his eyes, and I doubted he'd even heard me. His shoulders curled forward, his lips moving with silent words. The curse was calling to him.

I was hoping she'd die from the knife I'd jabbed into her gut, but the thing about fae was that they were resilient when it came to not dying. That whole eternal life thing they had going.

Clouds thickened overhead, briskly darkening the sky with a promise of rain. Another reason to hurry. We made our way along the river's bank, the soft roar of the upcoming waterfall growing louder the closer we got.

"So, what's the plan?" he snapped suddenly, looking at me with glazed-over eyes. "I go for a swim?"

"Yeah, something like that. I need to make sure you're cleansed before you go back near Rune. You've already done enough damage."

He cut me a sharp glare, guilt flickering in his gaze at the mention of Rune. "Why are we still walking if I just have to get wet in the river?" He stared at the water we traipsed past.

"Just keep moving. It has to be just the right spot."

It wasn't long before we stood on a rock's edge near the waterfall that thundered, blotting out Wilder's angry words. He was acting like Dr. Jekyll and Mr. Hyde and starting to piss me off. But by the way he was shaking his head and pointing to the cliff at our feet, I guessed he was either asking me why I had brought him up here or telling me that he wasn't going down there. Could be anyone's guess since I wasn't really listening to him.

"What do you see down there?" I yelled, pointing at the pristine water where I'd brought Rune for a swim days ago.

Wilder's gaze followed mine and turned to stare down at the clear water.

Suddenly, I grinned, flexed my muscles, and shoved my hands into his back.

He tumbled right off the cliff.

He bellowed, pumping his arms and legs in the air.

"Don't be such a baby, it's not that far down," I yelled after him. It was maybe fifty feet.

He hit the splashing water just where the waterfall crashed. Sure, I didn't need to throw him off the cliff, and he could have just as easily walked into the river to be dunked under and cleansed. But where would the fun be with that? Plus, I needed to shake him the fuck up.

He stayed under there a bit longer than he should have. What the hell, Wilder? I was certain he could swim... He better not have hit his head. I'd be super pissed if he made me dive in to save his ass.

I scanned the water, getting antsy. Rune would never forgive me for killing Wilder, this I knew.

Eventually, he burst out from under the surface, splashing around like a drowning rat, gasping for air. I exhaled loudly. Goddamnit.

"You fucking asshole," he shouted. "I could have died."

"But you didn't. How are you feeling?" I yelled back over the roaring waterfall.

Even from up here, I could see his eyes narrowing at me with anger. Then he gave me the finger. Okay, well, it seemed like Wilder was back.

"I'll collect the car and come grab you," I told him, unsure if he had heard me, then walked off as he screamed curses at me. I wasn't sure which side of him I preferred.

The doped-up version or the one where he went ape-shit over everything?

The main thing was, Rune would be ecstatic, and that was all that mattered to me.

Rune

The day reflected the mood, dark and gloomy. I stood in the cemetery at the site that Miyu had picked to bury Rae. Besides Miyu, it was only the preacher, Miyu's aunt, Daxon, Wilder, and me.

I was surprised that Wilder had shown up. We hadn't spoken since he'd left while I was sleeping. Wilder kept shooting me furtive looks like he wanted to say something, but every time he opened his mouth, he would look at the others gathered around and stay silent.

I didn't mind that. I didn't need any more sadness today.

Word had somehow leaked out that Rae was responsible for the murders, and everyone from town seemed to have collectively decided that they wouldn't be paying any respects. I was hurt and angry on Miyu's behalf, especially after finding out that he had probably been poisoned. I would have at least thought that Miyu's friends would have shown up to support her, but they evidently hadn't felt the same.

Miyu didn't seem to care that no one else was here, though. She stood stiffly by the mound of dirt, tears streaking her face as the preacher talked about the better life that Rae had waiting for him. He at least was pretending that the person he was burying hadn't murdered anyone.

The preacher began talking about how the ones Rae had left behind would have to carry on, and Miyu lost it, her soft tears turning into hiccupped hysterics as she fell to her knees, the mud from the last few days of rain sinking into her dress.

I couldn't control my tears either as I watched my friend fall apart. The preacher finally ended his sermon and nodded to us before kneeling down to say a few whispered words to Miyu who was still on the ground. Miyu nodded at whatever he said, and then he stood up and smiled somberly at us before leaving, rather quickly I noticed.

There was a rose flower arrangement by the headstone that Daxon and I had bought, and Miyu stood up and walked over to pick one of the roses. She brought it over to the mound of dirt and stared down at it.

I saw Daxon and Wilder walking away, trying to give Miyu some space. I hovered nearby, just in case she needed me. Miyu's aunt stayed in her seat, watching Miyu closely like she was prepared to jump in and save her at any time.

"I'm sorry that I didn't see it sooner, that I didn't do something. I'm sorry that I failed you," she whispered, her hand trailing along the headstone that read "Beloved Love, Beloved Mate, Beloved Forever." It might have been the most heartbreaking thing I'd ever read.

The temperature in the air suddenly dipped, like a cold front had moved in that instant. Rae's form appeared right in front of Miyu, and I stiffened, hoping that we weren't wrong about who he really was and he wasn't going to attack.

But Rae just stood there, his face the picture of despair as he stared at Miyu like she was his world.

All of a sudden, her face went slack, and she sighed as if in relief. "Rae," she murmured.

She could sense him.

Miyu looked over at me. "He's here, isn't he?" she murmured.

I nodded, too choked up to be able to talk.

She held up her hand in the air, and I watched as Rae lifted his hand up to meet hers. Miyu leaned her face forward, and he matched the movement until their foreheads were touching.

"Thank you for loving me, and making me believe in love again," she whispered. Tears streamed down his face, and his whole body shook as he stood there.

"Can you talk for me?" he asked, not looking over at me.

"Yes," I whispered.

"Can you tell her to still believe in happy endings, and that I know she's going to have a great life."

I failed at holding in a hiccuped sob. "Miyu, he wants me to tell you that he wants you to still believe in happy endings, and that you're going to have a great life."

Her body shook as she cried. "How will that be possible? You were supposed to be my happy ending, Rae."

He closed his eyes as more ghostly tears leaked out. "I've gotten a glimpse of her future, and it's going to be beautiful. She just has to get through this hard part first," he whispered.

I repeated what he said, and she shook her head frantically. "I don't want that. I just want you back. Please, come back."

"I love you, Miyu. In any lifetime, I would have chosen you, no matter what. Goodbye, my love."

His form started to evaporate, and I saw a look of peace in his eyes that hadn't been present before as he faded away. He never took his eyes off her as he disappeared.

And then he was gone. This time, I suspected, for good.

"He's gone," she whimpered as she sank to her knees.

I told her what he'd said, about choosing her no matter what, and that only made it worse.

"That's what he used to tell me when I was scared because I wasn't his fated mate. That's what he would tell me to get through my fear. And now it doesn't even matter."

I didn't have anything to say to that.

Because maybe she was right.

———

Miyu held a small reception at her house, and some of her friends did come for that. They gave her hollow smiles and stiff hugs, like they were ashamed to be there, but she gripped onto them tightly nevertheless.

When most everyone had left, I began to gather up some trash as she walked out to the back patio and stared up at the moon. Seems we'd both been doing that quite a bit as of late.

After I got the living room and kitchen area cleaned up, Miyu's aunt went to work on the dining area, and I walked outside to join Miyu.

"How are you feeling?" I asked as I put an arm around her, and she leaned her head on mine.

"I'm going to have to leave, Rune," she murmured.

"What?" I asked, even though the words shouldn't have come as that big of a surprise. I knew all about running away, after all.

"He's everywhere. He's all over this house, all over this town. I—just can't stand it. I can't stand to constantly be reminded of what I've lost."

"But what about finding out who poisoned him?" I

asked hesitantly. She'd seemed to be so bent on finding out the truth before.

"Does it really matter?" she asked sadly. "You know the people in this town. They're never going to change their minds about him. They couldn't even come out and support me, like I'm guilty by association, I guess." She sighed, a solitary tear trailing down her cheek. "No matter what, it won't bring him back. And I don't know how to exist without him. So I think I need to leave until I can figure that out."

"I'll miss you so much," I told her, squeezing her tight.

"I'll miss you too, Rune. You're the best friend that I've ever had. That won't change just because I'm not here."

We stayed there, looking up at the moon for a long time.

And the next morning...she left with a tear-filled goodbye.

It was awful and sad, and I hoped she found what she was looking for out there.

I was still hoping I could find it myself.

14

WILDER

I didn't know if I was ever going to get Rune to forgive me for what happened with Daria, but I wouldn't stop trying, no matter how long it took.

Starting with tonight.

Ares was going to die at a little dinner party we were holding tonight. We of course hadn't told Rune that because she seemed to have developed a soft spot for the guy. But he had to go. Daxon and I were both in 100% agreement about that.

As soon as I had hit the water over the waterfall, the fog and pain I'd been dealing with constantly had disappeared. Everything involving my feelings for Rune had become crystal clear. The overwhelming love and complete devotion had hit me, flaying my insides with regret at what had transpired with Daria.

I remembered it now. I'd remembered leaving Rune with words I didn't mean, hurt battering my ribs as I marched out into the night. I'd been about to shift when Daria happened into the glen I was standing in. And of course, right then she'd decided to call in my debt for helping Rune.

It was only supposed to be a kiss, a meaningless kiss. You couldn't break a vow with a fae; after all, it meant immediate death. But I thought it would be alright.

Daria obviously must have put a spell on her lips, because everything was different after our lips touched. She'd all of a sudden been the love of my life, the woman I'd let slip away, my entire future.

It was a testament to my feelings for Rune that she'd been able to slip through the cracks of the spell. My wolf hadn't fallen prey to the spell. He considered Rune his mate, and evidently, there was no magic, even powerful fae magic, that could change that.

Thank god.

On the agenda for the evening, after getting rid of Ares of course, was talking to Rune. It literally killed me seeing her at the funeral and not being able to say anything.

Daxon had said that Rune still loved me, and everything from our night together had seemed to confirm that, but when would it be too much? When would she get tired of all the assholes in her life constantly hurting her and decide to jump ship?

Hopefully that point wasn't now, because as I'd burst to the surface in that absurdly pleasant water Daxon had thrown me in, I'd sent a thousand prayers to the Moon Goddess to give me another chance with Rune. I'd promised her anything that she wanted from me. Which I guess, after my experience with Daria, probably wasn't the smartest thing, but I had to have faith that the Moon Goddess was as wonderful as we'd always been told she was.

"Did you get it?" Daxon asked as he strode through the

front door. This was his house after all, but the asshole could have at least said hello.

Not that he owed me anything. A part of me still couldn't believe that he had helped me when I'd left the perfect opening for him to have Rune himself.

I didn't know that I would have been unselfish enough to do the same in his position.

Fuck, who would have thought the psychopath would have been the better man for Rune after all.

"I got it," I responded, walking over to the table and gently picking up the small chest I'd retrieved from the secret room under the town hall. We would try to snap his neck first, of course, or tear his throat out. But if that didn't work, since we weren't quite sure what kind of supernatural he was, this would have to do the trick.

Under the town hall was a room only known to the alphas of Amarok. It was filled to the brim with all sorts of supernatural items that the leaders had collected since the town's founding, however many hundreds of years ago. There were about twenty different locks that had to be undone to get into the room, both magical and the normal kind. Sometimes I woke up in the middle of the night at the thought of someone getting into that room.

And what I had in my hand was from that room. A poison guaranteed to kill any supernatural on earth.

It might have been overkill, but there was just something about Ares. You could feel the power radiating off of him. He had to go.

Daxon lifted the lid to the chest to look at the crimson powder. "Perfect."

One of the caterers came out of the kitchen to tell us that the food was almost ready, and Daxon snapped the lid closed before giving them a charming smile.

Psycho.

"What time is Rune coming?" I asked Daxon, like the coward I was. I should have reached out already, but I was so scared she wouldn't talk to me that I hadn't even bothered to call her.

"In about twenty minutes," Daxon responded with a smirk, loving seeing me uncomfortable.

I blew out a breath and glanced in the mirror of the hallway, making sure I looked okay. Fuck, who was I right now?

A knock sounded on the door--the party was beginning.

We'd invited all of our betas, and a few of the other town power players, all under the guise of welcoming our charming new visitor to the town. Ares had mentioned to several people that he planned to stay awhile, and since everyone seemed to love him, having a dinner like this wouldn't seem that out of the ordinary even with the town's wariness of strangers...a wariness which evidently didn't apply to Ares.

It wouldn't be that strange when he disappeared, since he was just a visitor. We would just tell people that he'd decided to move on and hadn't been big on goodbyes.

The man of the hour arrived just then...with Rune.

The bastard grinned broadly when I opened the door, knowing that it would drive me crazy to see him with her even though he wouldn't have known that Rune and I weren't exactly on the best of terms at the moment.

"Wilder," Rune said in surprise.

"Hi, sweetheart," I murmured, and she blushed, hope and wariness at war in her gaze.

"I happened to walk up right as our guest of honor was arriving," she explained.

Since I was going to be killing him later, I just smiled

politely at Ares and pretended I didn't have a care in the world as I stood aside to allow them both to come in.

"Right this way. We're glad you could make it tonight," I tell Ares, putting my arm around Rune's waist possessively. Ares eyed my hand, and the way it was clutching at a confused-looking Rune, with a twinkle in his eye.

This guy couldn't die soon enough.

Fuck. I was turning into Daxon.

I led them into the main living area where servers were walking around the room with trays of appetizers for the guests. The town used to have small get-togethers like this all the time when our fathers were the Alphas, but this was actually the first time Daxon and I had put something like this together.

Knowing both of our fathers, I assumed that they also had murder on the agenda at many of their gatherings as well.

I led Ares over to where Daxon was standing, still keeping my arm around Rune. "Daxon, why don't you get Ares a drink while I talk to Rune for a moment," I prompted. We didn't want to poison him until the end of the night, but if we could get him drunk beforehand, it would definitely make things easier.

"Do you like Whiskey Sours?" Daxon asked with a friendly grin as he clapped a still amused-looking Ares on the back.

I led Rune away before he answered, practically carrying her down the hall in my eagerness to talk to her.

I tried to smile and nod at curious-looking guests as we passed, but I was sure my smile looked more like a pained grimace.

As soon as we got away from prying eyes, I had Rune

against the wall and started devouring her lips like my life depended on it.

Fuck. How had I ever stayed away? She tasted so good, it was hard to comprehend any spell working well enough to make me forget this. How I felt about her. How she was everything to me.

She pressed on my chest, pushing and pulling at my shirt simultaneously as if she couldn't decide what she wanted to do with me. Finally, she ripped her lips away from mine.

"Wilder, what are you doing?" she gasped, her chest rising and falling rapidly from the passion of our kiss.

She was so fucking beautiful. The most beautiful creature I'd ever seen. Her lips were swollen and shiny from our kiss, and her cheeks were a delicious rosy hue. Fuck me. She was perfect.

"Daria had me under an enchantment. I ran into her after I left that night, and she cast some kind of love spell. I never in a million years would have ever done something like that on my own. I know what I said that night, but I didn't mean any of it. I was just being an asshole, and then I ran into Daria and fuck—Rune, please forgive me. I'll do anything. I love you so fucking much. You're everything to me. And even under a spell, my wolf still knew that—I still knew that." My words came out in a rush, desperation embedded into every syllable.

Rune stared at me unblinkingly, her mouth slightly open as if she couldn't understand a word that I was saying.

I hesitantly brushed my fingertips across her face. I'd just had my mouth all over hers, but I was terrified now that she was going to reject me.

"It was all just a spell from that horrible woman?" she

finally said, her lips trembling and her eyes welling up with tears.

"Yes, baby. I—I don't know how I'll ever be able to make anything up to you. I don't deserve any of your—" My words were cut off as she threw her arms around me and pressed her lips against mine.

"I thought I'd lost you. Even that night, you were there, but you weren't at the same time. I've been so desperate for you. I love you so much," she said through her tears as she pressed kisses all over my face. "I kept thinking it was a bad dream and that I would eventually wake up. My heart couldn't believe that I'd lost you. I've been so lost without you."

My heart leaped in my chest, and I felt like the freaking Grinch because I swore my heart grew at least three sizes right then and there. I bit my cheek, knowing that I needed to tell her everything.

"The spell started because I kissed her," I told her. "That night, I had gone to shift and she was suddenly there, calling in the favor that she'd claimed when she masked your scent. I—I thought it would just be a small kiss, that it would be nothing. But obviously, I'm an idiot because you never come out ahead with a fae, and I'm so fucking sorry." I was rattling on, my insides shaking at the combination of having her in my arms again and admitting my sins.

"I don't know that there's anything you could do that could make me stop loving you," she said solemnly, a hint of heartbreak still there in those beautiful blue eyes of hers.

I squeezed my eyes shut, knowing I needed to admit one more sin to her. "It was just supposed to be a kiss, but I think a part of me wanted to know if she could make me feel something, make me forget you because I was so upset."

"Did she make you feel something? I mean, we already know that she did make you forget me," she said with a small smile that I couldn't help but snort at. "But did she make you feel what you were looking for?"

"She didn't make me feel anything but disgust, at myself, at her...and then everything went hazy after that." I pulled her close to me, so close that we were just a whisper away and our foreheads were almost touching. "I'll take you any way I can have you, Rune. Even if it means sharing with Daxon. I know now a world without you, and I never want to experience it again. Please say you can forgive me."

"There's nothing to forgive, Wilder. What I'm asking of both of you is unfair-"

"But it's not. I realize that now. This whole time I've been thinking that you couldn't love me as much as I loved you, but that night...fuck that night. Even under her enchantment, I felt your heart. I could feel your love surrounding me. I don't know how it's possible to love two people with your whole heart, but somehow you've managed it." I chuckled softly, rubbing my nose against her tenderly and making her grin. "But I should have known you'd be capable of it."

"This is all very touching, but dinner's ready, you two," Daxon commented from nearby. I bared my teeth at where he was leaning against the wall, looking jealous and amused all at once.

Rune giggled before burying her face in my shirt and squeezing me tightly once more. I was desperate to get inside of her, but I guess murder was calling.

"Wait, how did you get rid of the spell?"

Daxon snorted, a very self-satisfied look on his face. "That would be me, princess. I couldn't really have you crying every day for the rest of our lives together over this asshole, could I?"

"You helped him?" she asked, looking at Daxon like he was freaking Santa Claus.

"Yes, Daxon did help in assisting me off the top of a waterfall into some kind of enchanted water," I said dryly.

"Any time," Daxon commented as Rune grabbed my hand and dragged me over to Daxon so she could give him a passionate kiss while still holding onto me tightly.

For a moment, with her in between us, my mind imagined a different scene. Of two different pairs of hands moving over her, two pairs of lips brushing against her skin...nope, we weren't going to go there.

Too soon.

A quick glance at Daxon's heated glare told me he might be thinking the same thing though.

Fuck.

Daxon and I both stepped away from her at the same moment, each of us deliberately not looking at the other.

"I love you both so much!" Rune cried, a brightness in her gaze. I wanted to figure out a way to keep it there forever.

"And we love you, baby. Forever," cooed Daxon as he gently guided her down the hallway to where the tables were set up for dinner.

Everyone looked at us expectantly as we walked in, and we quickly made our way to the three open seats in the center of the table, sitting with Rune in between us and Ares right across from us. Ares's gaze immediately locked on Rune and hardly ever strayed away, even when others at the table were trying to talk to us.

The company Daxon had hired to cater the dinner was a local one, of course, and they'd done an amazing job, or at least I thought they did. Now that things were patched up with Rune, everything seemed to taste amazing. I was pretty sure the fucking oxygen I was breathing tasted better as well. I dug into my steak, making sure to get some garlic mashed potatoes with my bite. I heard Rune moan softly next to me, and I instantly hardened, trying not to glare at Ares too hard when arousal spiked in his gaze as well, since he'd been listening to her.

"So, Rune, have any plans for the holidays?" Ares asked with a soft smile.

I gritted my teeth when she gave him one back.

Rune bit her lip and shrugged. "I haven't really celebrated Christmas lately, so anything will be awesome," she said softly.

I heard Daxon growl under his breath at the reminder of what our little wolf had gone through.

"I heard that the farm down the road does carriage rides. We'll have to go," he told her.

Rune shifted uncomfortably next to us, most likely having no idea that he was asking her out for a date right in front of us.

"That sounds great. I'm sure we would all like to go," responded Daxon as he stuffed a big bite of steak into his mouth.

I couldn't stop the laugh that slipped out as Ares's gaze hardened for a brief moment before he pushed a charming smile forward. It was that brief slip of his mask, though, that reminded me how dangerous he was. There hadn't been just anger in his gaze...there'd also been a touch of madness.

We let the other guests take over the conversation with Ares until most everyone had finished dinner.

And then it was toast time.

Daxon slipped away to the kitchens to make sure the poison was put in one of those glasses, and then he led the procession of waiters out into the dining area, holding a tray that contained regular champagne glasses along with the bejeweled glass that had been used for guests of honor in our pack for at least a hundred years.

Pretty convenient to make sure the poison wasn't given to the wrong person.

Daxon handed out the tray of drinks to our table while the waiters took care of the rest of our guests.

Daxon's smile looked a bit too sinister as he handed Ares his glass, but Ares didn't seem to notice, so maybe that was just in my imagination.

"Let's all raise our glasses for our visitor, Ares Bain. He's won the hearts of practically the whole town already, and we're lucky to have him," Daxon announced, raising his champagne glass as the whole room sickeningly cheered.

Seriously. Who were these townspeople that I could always count on to be just as suspicious of strangers as Daxon and I were?

Ares kept his gaze locked on Rune as he took a big sip from his special glass. The poison didn't take long to work, or at least that's what we'd been told when we'd first gotten access to that secret room and all of its treasures.

The party really needed to end just in case he decided to drop dead quickly.

As elegantly as we could, we ushered out the guests, sending them home with little goodie bags of treats that we'd been told by the caterers would be a big hit. The air in front of Daxon's house was filled with laughter and excited talking as the guests walked out into the brisk night. Unfortunately, Rune was one of those guests leaving. She couldn't exactly be around while we were plotting the murder of a man she thought was just a nice stranger...or worse, a friend. Daxon had already killed enough of her friends.

We'd convinced Rune that she didn't need to help clean up and that she should go to the inn with Carrie. One of us would join her later...preferably me, of course. She had left with a slight frown but no outward suspicion.

After the cleaning crew left, it was just us and Ares, who we'd told to stay for a nightcap.

He stood there chatting with Daxon while I watched, hoping he'd die quickly.

"Quite the party you threw tonight, gentleman," Ares said as he sipped at his whiskey sour. I'd seen Daxon sprinkle a bit of powder into that drink as well for good measure.

I'd prepared my own drink...just in case.

"I think you'll find this town's always up for a celebration. One of the many great things about a small town," I commented.

Can you please just die already?

Thirty minutes later, after an inane conversation so boring and fake my ears wanted to bleed, his face went slack and he collapsed to the ground without another word.

"Finally," Daxon groaned. "That guy really likes to hear himself talk. I thought it was never going to end."

"Tell me about it," I agreed as I stooped down to check his pulse.

Not a beat could be felt.

"I'll stab him when we get there to make sure he's dead. I just had these floors cleaned," Daxon commented calmly, as if he was discussing the weather. I rolled my eyes and picked up Ares's legs while Daxon grabbed his arms and began to head towards the garage and his car.

We threw Ares into the backseat and then we took off to a farmer's property that was an hour away.

A farmer who happened to have at least a hundred hogs that the farmer was fine with being creatively fed. For a fee, of course.

Daxon *was* the one who had arranged it.

Fucking psychopath.

Daxon normally would have taken him into his basement of horror, but he was evidently a bit scarred from Rune walking in on him with Rae, and this was apparently the next best way to get rid of a body.

We didn't talk much on the drive. Daxon had classical music playing that was honestly a bit terrifying sounding, and he kept tapping along with the beat of the music on the steering wheel. I was just about to the point where I was thinking of stabbing Daxon just to get him to stop when we turned left and headed up an unlit long gravel drive that reminded me of something out of *Texas Chainsaw Massacre*.

The gravel road stretched at least another mile before I finally saw a huge metal pen appear in the distance. When we finally got to the metal fence, Daxon stopped the car and we both got out. Daxon was fucking whistling as he opened his trunk and pulled some black tarp out. He then laid it on the ground, and we pulled Ares's body out of the car and onto the tarp. Daxon then pulled a long, jagged-edged knife out from under his backseat and promptly stabbed Ares in the heart. Ares didn't even flinch, so apparently, he was still dead.

I took the knife from Daxon and sliced it across Ares's throat. Just for good measure.

Daxon threw me a bright grin like we were fucking bonding or something, and then we both pulled the tarp over to where the sadistic hogs were waiting for us.

"Ready?" Daxon asked with a grin, obviously loving this.

I grimaced and nodded as we heaved the tarp and body over the fence.

It was literally only a minute before the hogs descended. I was pretty sure the sound of them eating and crunching bones would haunt my dreams, but they were very effective little monsters.

Daxon made us stay and listen for the longest ten minutes of my life as they ate, and then we were back in the car, hopefully headed to Rune...after making sure we didn't smell like pigs, of course.

"Nice working with you, buddy," Daxon smirked, and I shook my head with a grimace before holding out my fist for him to bump...like the friends we evidently were.

Friends was probably too strong of a word. We'd call it partners for now, even if I owed him my life for bringing me back to Rune.

At least we had one problem down...

15

RUNE

The sudden boom of giggling flooded the diner, snatching my attention from my plate of scrambled eggs and avocado on toast.

Greta, the town gossip, was making sounds that should be coming from a schoolgirl crushing over the new guy in her class. Instead, the older woman stood near the doorway, chatting with Ares who held the door open for her to leave. The way he stared at her, grinning, his attention wholeheartedly on her, could make any girl melt.

It was one of a myriad of observations I made when I watched him. Like the way he ran his hand through his hair when he wanted to distract you, or that he had a tendency to reach out and touch you, just enough to make you buzz. Just as he was doing right now to Greta, and instantly, her eyes lit up. The guy knew how to captivate you. And somehow, he'd managed to cast his spell over most in town.

Including me, seeing as how my first reaction came in the form of butterflies beating wildly in my stomach in his presence. Something about him made me ridiculously excited, and suddenly *I* felt like the schoolgirl getting all giddy over the new guy.

Greta finally walked out of the diner, still staring at Ares over her shoulder, giggling again, and I rolled my eyes. But then again, Ares carried an air about him that made you pause and stare. He was insanely handsome, tall, dark, and mysterious... The whole package, complete with the promise of a perfect body as evidenced by the muscles bulging out from under his black shirt.

When he looked around, our gazes clashed and the corners of his mouth curled upward. I dropped my gaze to my breakfast like I'd been caught with my hand in the cookie jar. I peered back up to see him sauntering over to me with confidence, flashing me his signature wink.

He had his sleeves rolled up to his elbows, and I wouldn't lie that when his dark gaze raked over me, I might have gotten slightly wet.

After last night's town party, I woke up with my stomach growling for food, so I came in early for my shift to have breakfast in peace.

Never in a hundred years did I expect Ares to come into the diner.

When he sat across from me, I wasn't surprised.

His mouth was pulled into a sensual smile, one that made my heart pitter-patter louder.

"Morning," he said, eyeing my plate of food. "If I had known you were here, I wouldn't have eaten breakfast already."

"You're missing out. I made these myself, and they are divine." I scooped a forkful of egg into my mouth.

"Are you the chef here?" he asked, his gaze falling to my chest. At first, I assumed he was checking me out, and my cheeks burned until I glanced down at my name tag.

Shaking my head, I said, "Just the waitress, but the new chef was running late this morning." As much as I tried to avoid it, Rae came to mind, along with how hard it was to work knowing he wouldn't be in the kitchen when I popped in there to collect meals. Instinctively, I lifted my gaze to the kitchen door, and I felt Ares' eyes on me.

"Do you want me to order you a coffee or something?" I asked.

"I'll get it. Can I order you anything else?"

"All good."

From the moment he got up and wandered over to the front register where Licia, the co-owner of the diner, was tidying the menus, my gaze dipped to his ass.

I shouldn't stare, but apparently, I was weak around him. Going back to my plate, I started eating quickly to distract myself.

At that moment, the side of my neck tingled, and I rubbed it, remembering my sleepwalking incident, how Ares had saved me. The rest of the night confused me... Maybe I completely dreamt the part about his lips on my neck, his touch like liquid fire on my skin. His whispered words that completely undid me. His bite that rendered me at his mercy. I'd had an actual orgasm. For an event that was a figment of my imagination, it shook me, left me dreaming of his mouth on me. His hard chest crushed against mine, hands sweeping across my body.

I rubbed the sensation on my neck and took another mouthful of breakfast, needing to get control over myself.

When Ares returned, that perfect smile greeted me again on full lips. I tried my hardest to tell myself the bite had all been in my mind because there was no mark on my neck when I woke up. But regardless, the sensations growing within me left me craving him.

"I meant to ask you how your wolf is," he asked, and his question took me off guard, leaving me perplexed about what he was talking about.

He must have seen the confusion on my face because he added, "When you were sleepwalking in the woods, I noticed you struggled with your wolf."

"Oh," I answered, my head running with so many thoughts, and I was left wondering how long he'd been watching me in the woods before coming to my rescue to notice that.

"She and I have just been working through some things," I answered as vaguely as possible. I barely understood what was happening to me. I didn't want to bring it up with a man I was still getting to know. If I learned anything, it was being cautious about who I trusted.

"So, what happened last night?" I asked, mostly to say something and stop the barrage of doubts in my mind. "You kicked everyone out pretty fast at the party last night."

Something amusing flashed over his gaze that I couldn't work out. "I had something to take care of. You looked spectacular though."

"Thank you," I answered and picked at my food, but I doubted I could eat another mouthful when every inch of me was aware of Ares sitting across the table from me. I sensed his eyes on me, just how far his hands were from me on the table. My chest clenched with an irresistible need to hold his attention. I felt like a desert, parched and desperate for water, while Ares was my oasis just out of reach.

Something must have been wrong with me to feel such intensity around him when I'd already given my heart to two other men.

"If I had more time last night, I would have shown you a hell of a night. One you wouldn't forget."

"You're awfully sure of yourself," I murmured with a smile.

He laughed, that hypnotic sound he made filling my ears and leaving me buzzing all over. To his credit, he didn't argue back and let me believe what I wanted. Was that part of his allure... saying just enough to entice me, so I filled in all the blanks.

"So, you said the other day you just got out of the army. Why aren't you traveling with a friend, or..." My throat dried, and I really was curious to find out if he had someone special in his life. Of course, I shouldn't care, and yet the question hung between us.

Licia arrived at our table just then and set a cup of coffee in front of Ares. She was fluttering her eyelashes, having only eyes for him. "Anything else I can get you, honey?" she practically purred the words.

Could she be any more obvious, just like nearly every other person in this town? But when she placed her hand on his shoulder, a low groan grazed over my throat from my wolf.

Down, girl. He isn't ours. What was that about anyway?

"This is perfect. Thank you," he answered with a soft voice.

Once Licia strolled back to the front of the diner to the new customers walking in, I noticed Ares smirking. "Is that your wolf happy to see me, or is she dying to rip into me?"

"She's just hungry," I lied, not wanting him to think there was anything else between us. "Anyway, tell me more about how everyone in town seems to be falling over themselves in your company."

Something in his eyes glinted. "Including you?"

I tried my best to act as nonchalantly as possible. "I'm not drooling all over you, am I?"

Instead of responding, he studied me and took a drink from his coffee. "I wish you would."

I burst out laughing at the way he lowered his voice, almost purring, trying to mimic Licia from earlier.

"I've always made friends easily," he said, straightening. "And like my general in the army used to tell me, I had an approachable face and personality. It makes people feel safe around me."

It was only then that I sensed someone watching me, and the hairs on the back of my neck lifted. It was a strange sensation.

I glanced over, and standing across the room was Daxon.

My heart gave a stuttering beat as a sliver of worry crawled through me. Except, he wasn't even paying attention to me. He glared at Ares.

Daxon's brow furrowed, lips pinched tight, and he kept rubbing his jawline. I really hoped this wouldn't be another repeat of them in the park, especially when more people entered the diner.

"Will you excuse me?" I said, shuffling out of my seat.

"It's perfectly fine, I was about to leave." Ares was on his feet too, and he leaned in close to me and whispered, "I'll be seeing you again very soon, Rune." Then he sauntered towards the door, glancing over to Daxon, giving him a friendly nod.

"Pleasant morning," Ares said to him, then strolled right out and headed up the sidewalk.

"The fuck..." Daxon muttered, and I swore his face had turned as white as a piece of paper.

I closed the distance between us in several quick steps and reached out, touching his arm. He looked down at me with eyes that appeared glazed over.

He seemed startled... almost as though he'd just seen a ghost.

"Are you okay?" I asked.

"H-how long has Ares been in the diner?" He couldn't stop looking at the door Ares had just walked out of moments earlier.

"Maybe ten or fifteen minutes. He just popped in for a coffee."

Daxon was shaking his head. "This can't fucking be," he murmured. He kept touching the base of his neck, his lips as pale as his face.

"Are you feeling sick?" I asked. "Maybe I can take you back home?"

His mouth opened but nothing came out. He was rapidly blinking, eyes fixated on the door. "How could this be?"

"Daxon, you're scaring me. What's going on?" I wasn't sure I could deal with Daxon now losing his mind. Couldn't things just settle down for a change?

When he finally turned toward me, his eyebrows were pressed together. "I need to go home, sweetheart. I'll catch up with you later."

Before I could even respond, he stormed right out of the diner, the door shutting hard behind him. He hadn't even kissed me.

Frustration flared in my gut because whatever Daxon was up to, I knew it would somehow come back to bite me.

"What was that about?" Licia interrupted my thoughts and paused next to me. "I've never seen Daxon so startled. What scared him? Or is he coming down with something?"

"I'm not really sure," I answered absentmindedly.

The front door bell rang as more customers walked in, and Licia hurried over to greet them while I struggled with the worry churning in my gut about Daxon's strange behavior after seeing Ares.

I made a mental note to check in on Daxon after my shift and find out what happened.

"Are you gonna stand there all day or get started with your shift?" Licia teased, pushing menus into my hands. "Table three is ready to place their order. Clean up your table too, and get a move on."

Glancing around, I'd noticed two full tables with customers settling down to order meals as well.

I nodded. "Absolutely." And I moved quickly to get to work.

Yet, I couldn't get Daxon's reaction to Ares out of my mind. He lacked his usual aggression and seemed more in shock, so something had definitely happened between them. And I was going to find out.

16

RUNE

I n the past couple of days, I'd come to the conclusion
that whatever was giving me nosebleeds when I
transformed, might be related to all the stress I'd been
under with Rae, Miyu, and Wilder.

A while ago, Miyu said something that got me thinking... *Your body can only take so much before it breaks down.*

So, what if this was my body's way of falling apart?
What if I'd pushed myself with stress to where I crippled
my own wolf?

And as such, I had a plan.

I moved quickly through the park, figuring I remained
close enough to town but not within view to have everyone
watch me struggle with my wolf. After spending the
morning following YouTube videos on meditation, I felt
ready to try again with the right state of mind.

Standing by the river, I sucked in a deep breath and shut
my eyes. Without rushing, I let myself reach for my wolf
within me. She stirred, brushing against my insides, letting
out a growl of frustration from being held back.

I know, I said in my mind. *Let's try this until we are both calm.*

Taking another inhale, I enjoyed the brisk breeze on my skin, listening to the birds chirping in the distance.

And I exhaled, relaxing my muscles, then called to my wolf.

She slid through me like water, so fluid that I knew she understood what I was doing.

I drew on her, imagined myself in wolf form... and she pushed forward.

A sharp ache cut across my middle and just as quickly shot through my body. I seized up, wincing, and I hugged myself to stop the stinging pain. My wolf withdrew, whining. *I'm sorry.* Opening my eyes, I rubbed the drip from my nose, and my fingers came back bloody.

Shit. What was wrong with me?

Without waiting, I tried again. I felt my wolf just below the surface, and she didn't seem suppressed, but something blocked her from coming out. This had to work.

After wiping the blood away with the tissues in my pocket, as I came prepared, I closed my eyes, stood by the water's edge, and tried again.

In that same moment, someone touched my arm.

I flinched, a small yelp in my throat as my eyes flipped open.

"Hey," Ares said, standing there with his gorgeous smile, and those midnight blue eyes greeting me like he was used to making women's panties melt with a single look. "Sorry to scare you."

I shook my head, and immediately in his presence, excitement awakened. He had this way of just making me forget everything and left me so giddy; I craved more of his company.

"I didn't hear you approaching. I was concentrating, trying to work with my wolf to give her some peace," I said.

"She's stuck, isn't she?" he asked, rubbing his chin.

"Is it that obvious?"

"Only because I saw you bleeding in the woods during your sleepwalking, and now again as you try to call to your wolf."

Chewing on my lower lip, I nodded. "There's no reason for her to be blocked, and my friend suggested it could be stress. So I'm trying to unblock her with a calm approach and—"

Without waiting for me to keep explaining, he leaned in and lowered his voice as though he was about to share a secret with me. "I don't think it's stress. You may have a small fae problem here."

I reared back, my gaze narrowing on him, while my thoughts flew to Daria. A sliver of panic crawled in my gut at that moment. What if it was connected to her? But she'd ran out of town after Daxon broke the spell she placed on Wilder.

I gave Ares a blank stare, refusing to let him see my shock. "What do you mean?"

"Rune, you've been spelled by a fae who put a clamp on your transformation ability. It's why you keep getting nose bleeds." He reached over and ran a finger over my upper lip, where I guessed I had more blood. And just as quickly, he put his thumb into his mouth.

That was strange, but I was too hung up on the whole fae spell to worry about him tasting my blood. "How would you know that? Are you a fae?" My mind was racing with scenarios.

"Rune," he began, reaching out to me, but I recoiled. "I'm not a fae, and I picked up on the magic when I was near you. I wasn't sure at first what I'd sensed, but when I saw you struggling just then, it all clicked into place."

I blinked at him, and I frowned with a huff. "Fuck! It was Daria!" I fumed. "Of course she would do that...and she's not going to remove it, not that she's even in town anymore," I rambled, mostly to myself. Then I lifted my gaze to Ares's. "I'm so sick and tired of everyone hurting me, using me for their own benefit. For suppressing my wolf when all I want is to live a normal life." I was trembling from the anger bubbling in my chest.

First Alistair, and then Daria. Who was next in line to try to hurt my wolf?

A gust of wind blew past. It was cold, promising a freezing winter.

"I'm sorry that happened to you," Ares said, his hand on my arm, rubbing the cold from me.

Darkness swallowed me. Wasn't it bad enough that Daria had tried to steal Wilder from me? And now there's this on top of it. With it, a desperation bloomed within me, clenching my throat, but I refused to play the victim anymore.

"I can help," Ares said, and I blinked up at him.

"How?" I held his stare. The last time I got my wolf back, it took a lot of effort.

Thunder tore through the air, and I flinched.

"I know someone who can remove spells. Someone who has done it before, because you'd be surprised how many people the fae curse." His words came out soft, and the tender way he stroked my arm left me staring into his piercing eyes. I was suddenly drowning in them. They were everything, like somehow they offered me solace from all my troubles.

Another roar thundered overhead, sounding like it was

going to war with the sky. Then the first patter of rain fell on my nose.

"Do you trust your friend?" I asked.

"Yes," he answered at once, without hesitation. "I should have said something earlier, but I wasn't sure what I'd sensed on you. Can I take you to them now and get them to help you?"

My head swam in so many directions, with going to Daxon and Wilder to tell them about this, or to get it fixed on my own. To protect myself and my wolf without taking more of my issues to my men. Especially after everything they'd been through as well.

"Where's your friend?" I asked

"Just out of town. It won't take long, but I'll take you only if you're comfortable with me escorting you there." He spoke so smoothly, and I couldn't help but smile while part of my brain wanted to respond that I'd go with him anywhere he asked.

Around me, the world had shrunk to just us two, no voices of locals in the distance, no thundering sounds. Just his mesmerizing gaze. Then his lips curled upward, and I floated in the calm energy he carried. He left me feeling light, breathless, and in complete awe of him.

"Are you ready, Rune?" he asked, his hand reaching out to me, palm upward, waiting for me to accept his offer. He looked hopeful, like somehow my acceptance would bring him immeasurable joy. And was it wrong that I wanted to make him happy? Or that I desperately needed to free my wolf?

My wolf growled in protest in my chest, while my hand reached out to accept him as if she had a will of her own.

Rain fell harder, big fat drops that drenched me quickly. Lightning seemed to split the heavens apart. It was as though the universe itself was urging me to accept Ares' help and get rid of the stupid fae spell.

My fingers grazed his, and he wrapped his fingers around mine. Then we were running through the torrential rain.

We'd rushed into his black Chevrolet Impala parked in a side alley two streets down from the grocery store. I hastily shut the door and burst out laughing at how wet I was. Every inch of me dripped in water, and when I looked over to Ares, I saw he wasn't faring any better.

"Wow, the weather turned bad fast," I said.

He smiled while water ran down his face. He wiped it away with his hand. "I love the rain. It helps wash away the pain."

"I like that," I responded while he leaned in between our seats and into the back, then returned with a small blanket.

"Dry and wrap yourself up so you don't catch a cold."

"Thanks." I did just that as he started the engine, which roared to life. Wiping my face, I ran the material over my hair and wrapped it around my shoulders, not even noticing that we'd left the town behind already. We turned onto the main road that led into town, and then we were cruising down the mountainous road.

Pulling the seat belt across myself, I stared outside where the rain pelted against the car, into the woodland. The windshield wipers zipped back and forth, making a slight whirring sound.

"Thank you," I said. "Especially since the weather is not the best for driving."

His hands worked the steering wheel seamlessly, even when the wind shoved against the car, sending us all over the road.

"I just wished I would have said something earlier." Instead of focusing completely on the road, he placed a hand on mine, which sat in my lap. Despite his cold touch, it comforted me.

"So tell me more about your friend. I probably should have asked before I just agreed so quickly," I said with a small laugh. "Are they a witch? Please tell me they won't be sacrificing a chicken or something," I teased.

He laughed, and I adored the magical sound he made. "Let's hope it doesn't come to that. But don't worry, I'll keep an eye out on you and make sure you're safe." A longing expression flared over his face. "It's actually nice to spend time with you on the drive."

The strange thing was, I couldn't agree more.

"Tell me more about where you grew up with your family, what you loved to do," he asked.

I settled back in my seat. Normally, I didn't enjoy talking about my parents because it all came with painful memories. But at that moment, a sense of nostalgia filled me, and I settled in my seat, telling him about how my mother would read me Harry Potter stories growing up, and that for a long time I believed fairy tales were real. I never mentioned Alastair or how quickly my mother had been to abandon me. Those memories remained buried deep in my mind, and if I could help it, they would be forgotten for all time.

I'd completely lost track of how long we'd traveled, talking about our favorite books and why I would love to discover a world like Harry Potter to live in, but when I looked at the clock on the dashboard, it flashed 12:03 p.m. I shook my head, convinced I was seeing the time incorrectly.

I had headed out to the park just after nine that morning. "I thought you said your friend lived close."

"If it wasn't raining and I didn't have to drive as slow as a snail behind all this traffic, we'd be there already." He gave me one of his winks that melted me into the seat and made me a puddle. How could this man be so handsome and affect me when I'd given my heart to Daxon and Wilder? Yet in his presence, I came undone, as though I had no will of my own.

"We're almost there," he said, taking a right-hand turn. We sped toward a town, leaving behind the main road.

Perhaps I should have been worried, but each time he looked at me with those eyes, I softened into my seat.

The homes of a town came into view. I eyed an older couple strolling on the sidewalk, carrying shopping bags. More of the houses we passed were small but run down and in dire need of fixing. A small girl played in the front yard of a dilapidated house with the window boarded up.

"What town are we in?" I asked.

"Clairevile. Ever since the local mining business shut down, many families left, and those who remain struggle to make ends meet."

"That's sad. Does that mean your friend will need payment? I didn't bring anything with me." It reminded me that I should tell my guys where I was in case they searched for me. I pulled out my cell phone from my pocket and quickly tapped a message to Wilder and Daxon, telling them I was with Ares in the town of Clairevile, and I wouldn't be too long. I also briefly said that my wolf has been blocked by Daria and Ares was helping me out. Maybe if they saw that Ares did something for me, they might see him as the good guy.

I noted the reception was patchy and hoped the message went through, then tucked the phone away.

"Who are you messaging?" he asked.

"Just Wilder and Daxon. They get worried if I vanish." I half smiled, to which Ares didn't seem to notice.

He turned down a narrow street flanked by high wooden fences. At the end, he turned right once more and then swung into the parking area of what looked like an old bar.

It was a large, wooden building, square in size, with a wrap-around porch. It almost had a western vibe going for it.

"Where are we, Ares?" I asked, a tremble curling around my words.

"Where we need to be." After turning off the engine, he got out of the car and came around to my side, then opened the door.

"Are you ready?" There was no softness to his words as there had been in the car, but I'd say it had everything to do with him getting wet from the rain.

When I climbed out and stared at the bar again, I noticed there were no signs or names on the place, but there was definitely movement behind the windows.

"Why are we at a bar? Is your friend here?"

He nodded and collected my hand in his, holding me tightly.

We're going to get help, I kept repeating in my mind as we hurried under the cover over the front door.

Ares pushed it open, and we entered a room that reeked of something stale and pungent. The dark wooden walls matched the ceiling. Deer heads covered the walls, and I could have sworn we'd just stepped into a hunter's lodge.

The chatter died instantly at our arrival.

I swallowed the boulder in my throat, scanning the bar at the back of the room. An older man was wiping down the counter, and to my right stood three doors, all shut.

At least a dozen men were staring at me, and my skin crawled. Huge, burly men who looked like they could wrestle bears if they wanted. Some dressed in camouflage clothing as if they'd just come back from a hunt, while others were in casual clothes like Ares—jeans and a t-shirt.

But they all carried the same gleam in their eyes as if suddenly, they'd found their prize prey.

Me.

I didn't like it here, and the urgency to get out consumed me. I needed to be anywhere else but there. And I kicked myself for not going to Wilder and Daxon first.

Thunder cracked outside once more, and the walls felt like they closed in around me.

"I-I think we should leave," I murmured at Ares, tugging on his arm, except he was pulling me deeper into the bar, his hold squeezing until it hurt.

When the door shut with a bang behind me, I jumped. Turning my head, I noticed a six-foot-six beast of a man standing there, arms crossed over his chest, guarding the exit.

A shudder zipped up my spine. "Ares, what's going on? You said someone would help me with the fae spell."

Ares pivoted to look at me, and in front of me, his face seemed to transform. Gone was the softness I'd been used to, replaced by someone who had experienced too much hardship in his time. Hatred reddened his eyes, and he didn't resemble the kind man who'd stumbled into town.

My heart surged at the sight and transformation.

I yanked my arm out of his grip. "Who are you?"

The rest of the men were on their feet, stepping closer, glaring at me like I was the monster in the room.

"Took you long enough to return with her," one of the men growled.

My heart hammered, breaths see-sawing from my lips. I felt trapped, just like the animals on the walls must have felt in their last minutes of life.

"Where am I?" I demanded.

Lifting his gaze, Ares smirked cruelly, his dark eyes seeming to take on a darker red glow. Just as I thought I'd seen in my sleepwalking dream... And that was when the truth smacked into me. That night hadn't been a dream, had it? Everything with Ares in the woods had been real.

Crap.

The room tilted from the panic pounding me, and I hugged myself, frantically searching for the best escape out of there. They said that when your life flashed before your eyes, you either ran or fought. Right then, my instincts and my wolf growled for me to run. That I stood no chance... Especially with my wolf still blocked.

Ares towered over me, his tongue dragging over his lips, and I caught the glint of white from his sharp teeth.

"You're scaring me, Ares. What the fuck is this about?"

With his chin high, he commanded the room with his presence alone. "I've been tracking you for a very long time, Your Highness," he snarled. "Now, it's time to pay with your life for everything your family took from me."

I reared back, recoiling a step, and a small gasp grazed over my throat. His harsh words echoed in my head. Highness?

"W-What are you talking about?"

My pulse thundered in my ears.

The men's cheers for my death crowded in, the noise deafening.

My hands shook, and I recoiled.

Ares took a step closer, lips peeled back, and bared his extending fangs. The men around us hissed, baring their fangs too.

Oh, fuck!

I shuddered at the sight of these vampires, and I cursed myself for never once suspecting Ares. He put me under his thrall, hadn't he? It was what I'd heard vampires did. It all made sense now, and I hated how easily I fell into his trap.

"You fucking bastard. I trusted you," I cried out, my fingers trembling against my stomach, my hands slick with sweat.

A sense of satisfaction roared to life in his eyes.

"The first time I bit you was to confirm your bloodline. And now... I'll be the last thing you see," his hoarse words threatened, and then he lunged.

He slammed into me. His teeth struck my throat so fast, I stood no chance.

And I screamed as his fangs tore into my neck.

Get your copy of Wild Soul today!

WILD SOUL
BOOK 5

Real Wolves Bite. Continue the Wild series...

Get your copy of Wild Soul today!

WILD SERIES

Wild Moon

Wild Heart

Wild Girl

Wild Love

Wild Soul

BONUS SCENE

Join C.R. Jane's and Mila Young's newsletters to receive a bonus scene of Daxon meeting Rune from his POV!!

DOWNLOAD YOUR FREE COPY HERE

ACKNOWLEDGMENTS

This series is so fun to write. We can literally hear the sounds of your kindles hitting the wall when you reach the end of the books and it's delightful...hehehe.

A huge thank you to our editor Jasmine Jordan who stayed up until all hours of the night to get this book done after we were delayed because of weeks of sickness. We couldn't have done it without her.

Another huge thanks to Summer, the best beta reader ever. We basically live for her commentary as she goes through these books. She's such a patient, amazing friend and we're lucky to have her.

A huge thank you to Caitlin who is the best support and friend a girl could have, and who I'm lucky enough to have as my PA as well.

More thanks to Anna and Sarah for their tireless efforts and help in keeping us organized.

And last but not least, a thank you to you. How incredible it is that you gift us with your time and attention over and over again and continue to read our books. We love you readers so so much!

REAL ALPHAS BITE

I'm not in the habit of stealing women.

They come to me. They beg and plead for a taste of my power. My brothers and I rule the pack, crushing all challengers and scaring the rest into submission.

We're the nightmares that wake you up screaming, the devils you crave.

We have everything, so we want for nothing.

Until she came along.

From the first moment I laid eyes on her, I knew she was mine....ours.

We took her swiftly in the middle of the night, stealing her out from under her fated mate's clutches.

She was only meant to be a play thing, a passing fancy.

So why do I find myself watching her as she sleeps, protecting her... falling for her?

An RH rejected mate book

Grab Your Copy of Real Alphas Bite Today!

BOOKS BY C.R. JANE

www.crjanebooks.com

The Fated Wings Series

First Impressions

Forgotten Specters

The Fallen One (a Fated Wings Novella)

Forbidden Queens

Frightful Beginnings (a Fated Wings Short Story)

Faded Realms

Faithless Dreams

Fabled Kingdoms

Fated Wings 8

The Rock God (a Fated Wings Novella)

The Darkest Curse Series

Forget Me

Lost Passions

The Sounds of Us Contemporary Series (complete series)

Remember Us This Way

Remember You This Way

Remember Me This Way

Broken Hearts Academy Series (complete duet)

Heartbreak Prince

Heartbreak Lover

Ugly Hearts Series Contemporary Series

Ugly Hearts

Mafia Wars Dark Contemporary Standalone

Ruining Dahlia

Hades Redemption Series

The Darkest Lover

The Darkest Kingdom

Monster & Me Duet Co-write with Mila Young

Monster's Plaything

Academy of Souls Co-write with Mila Young (complete series)

School of Broken Souls

School of Broken Hearts

School of Broken Dreams

School of Broken Wings

Fallen World Series Co-write with Mila Young (complete series)

Bound

Broken

Betrayed

Thief of Hearts Co-write with Mila Young (complete series)

Siren Condemned

Siren Sacrificed

Siren Awakened

Siren Redeemed

Kingdom of Wolves Co-write with Mila Young

Wild Moon

Wild Heart

Wild Girl

Wild Love

Wild Soul

Stupid Boys Series Co-write with Rebecca Royce

Stupid Boys

Dumb Girl

Crazy Love

Breathe Me Duet Co-write with Ivy Fox (complete)

Breathe Me

Breathe You

Rich Demons of Darkwood Series Co-write with May Dawson

Make Me Lie

Make Me Beg

ABOUT C.R. JANE

A Texas girl living in Utah now, I'm a wife, mother, lawyer, and now author. My stories have been floating around in my head for years, and it has been a relief to finally get them down on paper. I'm a huge Dallas Cowboys fan and I primarily listen to Beyonce and Taylor Swift...don't lie and say you don't too.

My love of reading started probably when I was three and with a faster than normal ability to read, I've devoured hundreds of thousands of books in my life. It only made sense that I would start to create my own worlds since I was always getting lost in others'.

I like heroines who have to grow in order to become badasses, happy endings, and swoon-worthy, devoted, (and hot) male characters. If this sounds like you, I'm pretty sure we'll be friends.

I'm so glad to have you on my team...check out the links below for ways to hang out with me and more of my books you can read!

Visit my **Facebook** page to get updates.

Visit my **Amazon Author** page.

Visit myWebsite.

Sign up for mynewsletter to stay updated on new releases, find out random facts about me, and get access to different points of view from my characters.

ABOUT MILA YOUNG

Best-selling author, Mila Young tackles everything with the zeal and bravado of the fairytale heroes she grew up reading about. She slays monsters, real and imaginary, like there's no tomorrow. By day she rocks a keyboard as a marketing extraordinaire. At night she battles with her mighty pen-sword, creating fairytale retellings, and sexy ever after tales. In her spare time, she loves pretending she's a mighty warrior, walks on the beach with her dogs, cuddling up with her cats, and devouring every fantasy tale she can get her pinkies on.

Ready to read more and more from Mila Young? Subscribe today here.

Join Mila's **Wicked Readers group** for exclusive content, latest news, and giveaway. Click here.

For more information...
milayoungauthor@gmail.com

Printed in Great Britain
by Amazon